09/22/2021

Rusty Bedsprings

By I.P. Knightly

'Memoirs of a bed wetter'

I got fired from my job for arranging the vegetables into various sexual positions. Apparently, that's 'misconduct' for a special needs teacher!

Apparently, 29% of pet owners let their pets sleep on the bed with them, so I figured that I'd give it a try. But then my fucking goldfish died!

I went to the liquor store on my bike today and I bought a bottle of vodka and put it in the basket on the front of my bike. Then, it occurred to me that if I fall, the bottle might break. So, I drank it all right there. It's a good thing that I did because I fell seven times on the way home!

After winning the game, I threw the ball into the crowd, just like they do on TV. Apparently, that's unacceptable in bowling!

I hired an Indonesian hooker and she kept saying, "Small penis, no problem, small penis, no problem!" I would have enjoyed that encounter a lot more, if she had had no penis at all!

My grandfather has the heart of a lion, and a lifetime ban from the local zoo!

What's the number one way that Polacks try to commit suicide? By jumping out of their basement windows!

A man sees a woman with big breasts on the street and he approaches her. He asks her, "Excuse me Miss, will you let me pay you one-thousand dollars to nibble on your breasts?" She thinks about it and then says, "Okay." They then go into a secluded alley. She opens up her blouse and the man rubs his face on the woman's breasts wildly for ten minutes. The woman then asks, "Aren't you going to bite my tits?" The man replies, "No! It's way too expensive!"

I was once a Russian roulette referee. I did an excellent job. None of the losers complained!

A girlfriend asks her boyfriend, "Does my ass look fat in these jeans?" The boyfriend responds, "Yes, but at least it draws attention away from your face!"

My neighbours are always listening to loud music… whether they like it or not!

What did Hitler say when they turned the lights out? "I can Nazi!"

I used to date twins. My friend asked me, "How could you tell them apart?" I said, "Well, Jane painted her fingernails pink and Joey had a cock!"

Want to hear a joke about my dick? Never mind, it's too long!

If you can't tell the difference between a spoon and a ladle, then you're fat!

I farted in front of my girlfriend, and she got really pissed off. Apparently, saying, "A little gas never killed anyone" is something that you shouldn't say to a Jewish girl!

My girlfriend admitted to me that she was born 'Christian'. So, I immediately broke up with her. It may come across as insensitive, but I've only loved her and known her as 'Christine!'

Michael J. Fox is great at making Martinis, but he sucks at stealing tambourines.

I was trying to Google, "How do I know if I have Alzheimer's disease?" Apparently, someone has already Googled that on my computer multiple times!

A husband calls his doctor and says, "Doc, I have a really big problem. My wife just came back from her doctor's appointment, and she can't remember whether she was diagnosed with Alzheimer's or AIDS." The doctor says, "Oooh, that's a doozey. But I think that I have a solution. Drive your wife out to the countryside and leave her there. If she finds her way back home, don't fuck her!"

A husband says to his wife, "I bet that you can't tell me something that can make me both happy and sad at the same time!" His wife responds, "Your dick is bigger than your brothers!"

A man is in the graveyard when he sees a man squatting next to a grave. He says to the guy, "Morning!" The guy responds, "No. I'm just taking a shit!"

Did you hear about the new drug for lesbians? "Tricoxagin."

What did the pedophile say when he got out of prison? "I feel like a kid again!"

What's the leading cause of dry skin? Towels!

Why can't you explain 'puns' to kleptomaniacs? Because they always take things, literally!

What's the last thing that goes through a bug's mind when it hits a windshield? It's asshole!

When you look very closely, all mirrors look like eyeballs!

Why are all Jewish men circumcised? Because Jewish women don't like anything unless it's at least 20% off!

Do you want to hear a tasty tofu recipe? First, you throw out the tofu, and then you cook a really juicy steak!

Today my girlfriend asked me if I would still love her if she were fat and ugly. Apparently, "Yes, I still love you" was the wrong answer.

What's black and blue and doesn't like to have sex? The little boy in the trunk of my car!

A son asks his dad, "What is an alcoholic?" The dad points and says, "Son, do you see those four trees over there? An alcoholic would see eight trees." The son says, "Um, dad, there are only two trees."

A husband and a wife are having dinner at a fancy restaurant. The wife spills some tomato sauce on her white blouse and says, "Oh no! I look like a pig!" Her husband nods, and says, "And… you spilled some tomato sauce on your blouse."

Why did Princess Diana cross the road? Because she wasn't wearing her seatbelt!

What do you call Stevie Wonder and Hellen Keller playing tennis against each other? 'Endless Love'.

I got my son a trampoline for his birthday. The ungrateful little bastard cried the whole time while sitting in his wheelchair!

Why don't blind people go skydiving? It scares the shit out of their eye seeing dogs!

How do you convert your dishwasher into a snowblower? Hand her the shovel!

Your Momma's so stupid that she starved to death in a grocery store!

It's amazing how one letter can change the whole meaning of a word. I once introduced myself as a 'racist' when I actually meant to say, 'rapist.'

Did you hear the results of the Egypt versus Ethiopia soccer game? Egypt 8, Ethiopia didn't!

How did Rhianna find out that Chris Brown was cheating on her? She found another woman's lipstick on his knuckles.

Why don't Mennonites have 'drivers-ed' and 'sex-ed' on the same day? It's too hard on the horse!

What is the German word for a bra? Stoppemfromfloppen!

What did the pirate say on his eightieth birthday? "Ayyyeee mateeey!"

Two guys are fishing, and they reel in a bottle. They open it and a genie comes out and grants them one wish. The one guy says, "I wish that this whole lake was beer." The lake becomes beer, and the genie vanishes. The second guy says, "You idiot! Now we're going to have to piss in the boat!"

Friends are like trees. They fall over if you hit them with an axe!

I asked my doctor for advice on how to lose weight. He said, "Don't eat anything fatty." I said, "Thanks!" My doctor replied, "You're welcome, Fatty!"

When Miley Cyrus licks a sledgehammer while being naked, it's art. When I do it, 'I'm wasted' and I get kicked out of the Home Depot!

What do mopeds and fat girls have in common? They're both fun to ride until your friends find out!

A plastic knife is perfect for when a person wants to make some cut marks on their food and get insanely frustrated at the same time!

Did you hear that Richard Simmons had his love handles surgically removed? He has no ears now. The poor bastard can't wear glasses!

Did you know that if you hold your ear up to a stranger's leg you can hear them say, "What the fuck are you doing!!??"

My dad sent me to a psychiatrist for wearing his bra and panties again.

What's the difference between a walrus and a fox? About seven drinks.

If you get tired of elderly relatives coming up to you at weddings and saying, "You'll be next", try doing the same to them at funerals!

A wife wants to spice things up in the bedroom because it's been a while. So, she goes to Victoria's Secret and sees this bra that she really likes, but it happens to come with these crotchless panties. She says to herself, "Hell, why not!" and she buys them. Then she goes home, gets in the shower, does her hair, puts on her perfume, and then puts on the outfit. She walks into the living room and see her husband sitting in the couch watching TV. She stands between her husband and the TV, puts one leg up onto the coffee table like Captain Morgan and points to her crotch and says, "Do you want some of this, big boy?" The husband screams out, "Fuck no! Look what it did to your underwear!"

I was sitting in traffic the other day, it's probably the reason that I got hit by a car!

What does a Polack's vacation postcard say? I'm having a wonderful time, where am I?

How do blondes turn on the light after sex? By opening the car door!

I'm emotionally constipated, I haven't given a shit in days!

Little Johnny is out walking with his father when a bum comes up and says to the dad, "Can you help sir? I haven't had a bite all day?" Then Little Johnny bites him!

My Irish grandfather worked in a whiskey distillery. One night while he was working late, he fell into a vat of whiskey, and after six hours he drowned. It really shouldn't have taken him that long to die but he got out of the vat three times to pee.

Beauty is a light switch away!

What do you call one hundred thousand Frenchmen with their hands up? The French Army.

How do you separate the men from the boys in the Catholic church? With a crowbar!

Why did God invent alcohol? To prevent the Irish from ruling the world!

There was a power outage at the Polish department store yesterday. Twenty people were trapped on the escalator.

I have flabby thighs. Fortunately, my stomach covers them!

Your ideal weight would match your height, if you were nine foot two!

Your Momma's so fat that when she was diagnosed with flesh eating disease, the doctors gave her forty-five years to live!

I found this marvelous stuff recently. It's sugar free, low in fat, and you can have as much as you want without putting on weight. Crack is great!

I saw some graffiti written on the wall in the ladies' room. It read, "MY HUSBAND FOLLOWS ME EVERYWHERE!" Written just below it was the phrase, "NO I DON'T!"

A patient says to her doctor, "Doctor, everyone is ignoring me!" The doctor then says to his staff, "Next please!"

If shit was white, then toilet paper should be brown.

A woman says to her doctor, "Kiss me! Kiss me, you handsome stud!" The doctor replies, "I can't. That would be unethical. To be honest, I shouldn't even be having sex with you right now..."

Last week I replaced every window in my house. Then I realized that I had a crack in my glasses!

A man is standing at a urinal when he notices he's being watched by a midget standing next to him. The midget then puts a small stepladder next to the man, climbs it, and proceeds to look at the man's cock and balls. "Don't be embarrassed," says the midget. "I'm a doctor and I couldn't help but notice that you have a slight swelling of your testicles. It's probably nothing to worry about, but would you mind if I examine them?" The man is a bit surprised at the request but tells the midget to go ahead. The midget grabs the man's balls with a tight grip and says, "Okay, now hand over your wallet or I'm going to jump!"

"If I told you that you had a beautiful body, would you hold it against me?"

Confucius say, "Never tell a man with a chainsaw that he has bad breath."

What do you call a man with no arms and no legs with a seagull on his head? Cliff.

How do you get a hippie out of the bathtub? Turn on the water!

I have a great diet. You're allowed to eat anything that you want, but you must eat it with naked fat people!

Yo momma's glasses are so thick that when she looks at a map, she sees people waving!

My doctor is so useless that he treated me for jaundice for five years before he realized that I was Chinese!

A man gets seated on a flight next to a beautiful woman who's reading a book on sexual statistics. The man asks her about the book. "It's very interesting," she says. "It says that American Indians have the longest penises and that Polish men have the thickest. By the way, my name is Jill. What's yours?" The man replies, "Tonto Kowalski."

What do gay horses eat? "Heyyyyyy." (Said in an effeminate tone)

What do lesbian horses eat? "HAY!!" (Said in a loud and harsh tone)

What do you have if you've got a moth ball in each hand? A really big moth!

A midget walks over to a pretty girl at a party and propositions her, "What do you say to a little fuck?" The girl replies, "Hello, Little Fuck!!"

I wish that my girlfriend had told me about the mirror on the ceiling in her bedroom. I took off my clothes and laid down on the bed to get ready for her while she was in the bathroom. The next thing that I know, I'm being attacked by a naked skydiver. I freaked out and got the hell out of there as fast as I could!

I tried some of that aphrodisiac rhino horn and it really worked. Rhinos are super sexy to me now.

What do you call a midget scaling down a prison wall? A little condescending!

Hypochondria is the only disease that I don't have!

How many rednecks does it take to eat a possum? Two. One to eat it and the other to watch for traffic.

Confucius say, "Man with itchy bum wake up with stinky finger!"

What do you have if you've got two little green balls in your fist? Kermit The Frog's undivided attention!

What do elephants use for vibrators? Epileptics!

Why do they have Astroturf at redneck football fields? To keep the cheerleaders from grazing!

Mrs. McCafferty was best known for her famous Boston bean soup. She was asked for her secret to success. She replied that she only uses 239 beans. The interviewer asks, "Why only 239 beans?" She responds, "Because one more would make the soup too farty!"

What's brown and sounds like a bell? "Dunnngggg!"

An American Indian man walks into a bar and asks for a drink. The bartender says, "Sorry, we don't serve Indians here." The man replies, "But I'm not an Indian." "Prove it", says the bartender. The man raises his hand, and asks, "How?"

What's the definition of 'dangerous carnival sex'? When a fat woman sits on your face, and you try to guess her weight!

What does a man with a twelve-inch penis have for breakfast? Well, today, I had bacon, eggs, and toast with orange juice and coffee.

What do you call a Polack who's using a chainsaw? "Stump-inski"

What is the proper language to refer to the King of Ethiopia? "Boy".

How do we know that Adam was white and not black? Have you ever tried to take a rib away from a black man?

Why do gay guys have moustaches? To cover up the stretch marks!

What is a transvestite's main objective on Saturday nights? To eat, drink, and be Mary.

On the night of their wedding, a couple goes into the newlywed's suite to consummate the marriage. The newlywed wife comes out of the bathroom dressed in a cat outfit. They get to business in bed, but then the wife has an asthma attack, and they both go to sleep. The next morning the wife apologizes for her asthma attack. The newlywed husband replies, "Thank God it was asthma, I thought that you were hissing at me!"

My cock is so big that I rent it to Africa to provide shade!

What do you call a man with no arms and no legs who just won the lottery? Rich.

Looking back on my childhood, I finally realized that my parents really didn't like me. They told me that I could only eat candy as long it was given to me by strangers!

A man was attacked by three gay men while visiting San Francisco. They pinned him to the ground and spent three hours styling his hair!

How do you know if your roommate is gay? His cock tastes like shit!

Did you hear about the gay midget? He came out of the cupboard.

Since I threw out my back, my doctor told me that I have to sit down to pee because I'm not supposed to lift anything heavy.

Why do Scotsmen wear kilts? Because zippers frighten the sheep.

Two policemen are walking the beat when one says to the other, "When I get home, I'm going straight upstairs and I'm going to tear off my wife's underwear." "Feeling frisky?" asks the other cop. "No," says the first cop, "Her underwear is tight on me and it's driving me nuts!"

Two lions are walking down the aisle of a grocery store. One of the lions says to the other, "Pretty quiet in here today, eh?"

Yo momma's so short that you can see her feet in her driver's license picture.

If you want your wife to pay attention to every word that you say, try talking in your sleep!

If you want to drive your wife crazy, don't talk in your sleep, just smile.

How can you tell if your husband is dead? The sex is the same, but you get to use the remote!

At my physical today my doctor examined my testicles and found two very small lumps. Luckily, it turned out that they were just my testicles.

"Mommy, mommy! What's a lesbian?" "Ask your father. She knows."

A husband says to his wife, "Put your coat on, I'm going to the bar." His wife replies, "That's very nice of you, are you taking me out for a drink?" The husband shouts back, "No! I'm turning the heat off while I'm gone!"

I woman asks her husband, "How come you don't ever call out my name while we're making love?" The husband replies, "I don't want to wake you."

Little Jonny and his buddy are out in the yard playing with their pet turtles. They decide to bet ten dollars on who has the fastest turtle. The turtle who gets to the cement retaining wall in the backyard first wins. Both boys put their turtles on the starting line. The buddy's turtle starts moving slowly towards the finish line, but Little Johnny's turtle doesn't move. His buddy says, "You're going to lose the bet, you bastard!" Little Johnny says, "No I'm not!", and then Little Johnny picks up his turtle and heaves him full force into the wall.

I'm sick and tired of these 'Amber Alerts'. Either they wake you up at three A.M. in the morning or they broadcast your license plate number to the whole country!

What did the bald guy say when he was given a comb for his birthday? "Thanks, I'll never part with this comb and my pubes will look delightful!"

My girlfriend and I watched three movies back-to-back. Thank God that I was the one facing the TV!

Knock, knock. Who's there? Owls say. Owls say who? Yes, they do!

I said to my dad, "What rhymes with orange?" He replied, "No it doesn't!"

A man walks into a doctor's office with a cucumber up his nose, a carrot in his right ear, and a banana in his left ear. He asks the doctor, "What's wrong with me?" The doctor replies, "You're not eating right!"

I called my boss and told him that I wouldn't be into work today because I'm sick. He said, "You don't sound sick, how sick are you really?" I said, "I'm fucking my neighbour's dog right now! Is that sick enough for you?!"

What do you call a frozen camel? Lost!

'Microwave'. A hand gesture made by a midget to say hello!

What do you call a really smart blonde? A golden retriever.

What do you call a man with no arms and no legs with a harelip lying naked in the bottom of your bathtub? Dwayne!

When a dog licks his balls in public, nobody bats an eye. But when I do it, people say, "You sick fuck, what the hell are you doing to your dog?"

A wife asks her husband, "Can you explain how this lipstick got on your collar?" The husband replies, "No, I can't. I distinctly remember taking my shirt off."

Why is divorce so expensive? Because it's worth it!

I bought my friend an elephant to put in his living room. He said, "Thank you." I replied, "Don't mention it!"

I am so sick of Millennials. All that they do is walk around and act like they rent the place!

My wife left me because I'm insecure. No wait! She's back! She just went to go get some coffee!

Two flies are sitting on a piece of shit when one of the flies' farts. The other fly shouts, "Hey, what the fuck! Can't you see that I'm trying to eat over here!"

A dyslexic man walks into a bra…

A woman on welfare has five boys, all named Jamal. How does she tell them apart? By their last names!

The angry wife of a coroner asks him, "Why in the world would you cheat on me?!" The husband replies, "She was on the table naked! What else could I do?" The wife relies, "The god-damned autopsy!"

Today I decided to burn a lot of calories. I found a fat kid and lit him on fire!

Why can't Stevie Wonder see his friends? Because he's married, and his wife is a BITCH!"

Sherlock Holmes and Dr. Watson went camping and pitched a tent under the stars and got into the tent and went to sleep in their sleeping bags. Sometime in the middle of the night Holmes woke up Dr. Watson and said, "Watson, look up at the sky and tell me what you see." Watson replied, "I see millions and millions of stars." Holmes said, "And what do you deduce from that?" Watson relied, "Well, if there are millions of stars and if even only a few of them have planets, it's quite likely that are some planets like Earth out there, and there might also be life on them." Holmes replied, "Watson! You idiot! It means that someone stole our tent!"

Roses are red, violets are blue, I'm schizophrenic, and so am I!

I'm sick and tired about the assumption that we rednecks fuck our sisters. My sister hasn't put out in months!

Your mom is so fat, that when she gets out of the car at the grocery store, all of the automatic doors open!

I was diagnosed with clinical depression the other day. It made me sad.

In scuba diving, why is it important to fall backwards off of the side of the boat? Because if you fell forwards, you would still be in the boat!

What did the kid with Down's syndrome get on his SAT's? Drool!

If your dog was barking at the back door, and your wife was knocking on the front door, who would you let in first? The dog, at least he shuts up when he gets in!

A Chinese woman walks into a bank and asks the teller why the interest rate on her saving's account has decreased. The teller responds, "Fluctuations." The Chinese woman screams out, "Fluck you Americans too!"

Your grandma's vagina is so gross that opening it is like pulling apart a grilled cheese sandwich!

What did the blonde girl say when she found out that she was pregnant? "I wonder if it's mine?!"

I was at a music concert with my friend. He said, "I have to piss like a racehorse, but it'll take me forever to get through the crowd to get to the porta-potty, what should I do?" I replied, "Just pee in the pocket of the guy next to you!" He asked, "Won't he notice?" I said, "You didn't notice it when I pissed in your pocket!"

Last night I gave my wife a 'German oven' in bed. It's the same as a 'Dutch oven', except that she's Jewish.

Did you hear about the Polish general who wanted to be buried at sea? Six men died digging his grave!

How do Millennials fireproof their homes? By not owning one!

My friend had recently watched a Chernobyl documentary. He had grown up there and he said that the documentary was complete bullshit. He was able to count six false facts on one hand!

What do Chinese people do on 'Erection Day?" They vote!

How do you know if your mechanic has just had sex? He has one clean finger!

Your mom is so stupid that she got fired from the dollar store. She couldn't remember the prices!

Why do Polish people carry a car door around with them on summer days? So, they can roll the window down if it gets too hot!

An old man says to his friend, "I just bought a new hearing aid for $15,000, but it was worth it!" His friend asks, "What kind is it?" The old man replies, "It's twelve thirty!"

Three years ago, I asked my crush out for dinner. Last week I asked her to marry me. She said 'no' both times!

I had to quit mt job as a personal trainer. After a few weeks, I decided that I wasn't fit or strong enough to do my job properly, so I handed in my 'too weak' notice!

How did Burger King get Dairy Queen pregnant? He forgot to wrap his Whopper!

What's red and bad for your teeth? A brick!

Did you hear about the guy that was half Italian and half Polish? He made himself an offer that he couldn't understand!

Say all that you want about Hitler, but he wasn't that bad of a guy, he killed himself!

Why did Helen Keller have holes in her face? Because she tried using a fork!

Why are redneck murders so hard to solve? Because all of their DNA is the same and there are no dental records!

I wish that you were my big toe, because then I would bang you on every piece of furniture in my house!

A bishop asks two of his nuns to paint a room in the church. They get everything ready, but then realize that they didn't bring their painting clothes with them, and they're forbidden to get their habits dirty. So, they decided to paint in the nude. While they were painting, there was a knock at the door. They both look at each other in shock and ask in unison, "Who's there?" The voice on the other side of the door says, "Blind man!" The nuns look at each other and decide, "Why not?" They say to the man, "Come in!" The guy walks through the door and says, "Nice tits ladies! Where do you want me to hang these blinds?"

Your mom is like a doorhandle. Everybody gets a turn!

What do you call a woman who is paralyzed from the waist down? Married!

What did the buffalo say to his son when he left the farm? Bison!

What do you call a psychic midget who has escaped from prison? A small medium at large!

What's the dumbest animal in the jungle? A polar bear!

Why do you never see pigs hiding in trees? Because they're really good at it!

A man walks into a pet store asks for a dozen bees. The clerk carefully counts thirteen bees onto the counter. "That's one too many", says the customer. The clerk replies, "It's a 'freebee'!"

What kind of file do you need to turn a 14-millimeter hole into a 40-millimeter hole? A pedophile.

So, I painted my laptop computer black, hoping that it would run faster. Now it doesn't work!

How do you make 'Holy water'? You boil the hell out of it!

I got fired from my job at the bank today. A little old lady asked me to check her balance, so, I shoved her, and she fell down and broke a hip!

Two cows are grazing in a field. One cow says to the other, "Do you ever worry about 'Mad Cow Disease'? The other cow responds, "Fuck no! I'm a helicopter!"

What's the difference between ignorance and apathy? "I don't know, and I don't care!"

A girl goes to the checkout aisle at the grocery store. She has three TV dinners, a small carton of milk, one apple and a small bag of cat food. The cashiers says to the girl, "Let me guess, you're single?" She responds, "Yes! How did you know?" The cashier says, "Because you're fucking ugly!"

Where do Scotsmen get virgin wool? From ugly sheep!

What does it mean if a man remembers the colour of a woman's eyes after their first date? She's got small tits!

My girlfriend told me that sex was better while on vacation. It wasn't the best post card that I've ever received.

A man in the supermarket reminded me of Michael Jackson the other day. He said, "Don't ever forget Michael Jackson!"

A wife goes to a psychiatrist with concerns about her husband. She says to the psychiatrist, "My husband is acting really weird. He drinks his morning coffee and then he eats the coffee mug, but he leaves the coffee mug handle." The psychiatrist says, "Yes, that's really weird, the handle is the best part!"

My wife kept accusing me of being a transvestite. I couldn't take it anymore, so, I packed up her things and left!

I hate it when I run out of toilet paper. I have to make the trip to the grocery store in really small steps!

A cannibal showed up late for his family dinner. He got the 'cold shoulder'.

What's the fastest way to stop an argument between two deaf people? Shut off the lights.

I called the suicide hotline in Iraq. The attendant got really excited and asked me if I could drive a truck!

I took away my ex-girlfriend's wheelchair. Guess who came crawling back to me?

If you need to break up with someone, the best place to do it is at McDonald's. There are no plates or glasses to break on your head, no sharp knives, or pointy forks, and you can always hide behind a fat kid!

A kid decided to burn his family home down. His dad was watching the house fire, with tears in his eyes. He put his arm around his wife and said, "That's arson!"

A woman gives birth to a baby. The doctor takes the baby and throws it against the wall, drop kicks it and slaps it silly. The mother starts freaking out and is held back by the nurses. The mother screams, "Whyyyyyyyy??!!" The doctor holds the baby upside down by its ankle and says, "Don't worry, I'm just fucking with you. Your baby was born dead!"

What's faster than a cheetah? A Jewish woman with a coupon for free ham!

How do you get one million followers? Run through Africa with a water bottle!

What does an Ethiopian family photo look like? A barcode!

"I'm not racist. My shadow is dark!"

Tell a person, "I have 'dog-jaw', and then point to your jaw and say, "Touch here." When they go to touch your jaw, attempt to bite their finger and bark loudly!

What's black and white and red and can't fit through a revolving door? A nun with a spear through her head!

What's a fun thing to do while you're bored at Walmart? Go into a fitting room and shout out, "There's no toilet paper in here!"

Yesterday, I asked my dog, "What's two minus two?" He said nothing.

My wife hates that I have no sense of direction, to the point that I couldn't take it anymore. So, I packed up my things and right!

I asked over one hundred women, "Which shampoo do you prefer?" Almost every one of them replied, "Who the fuck are you and how the hell did you get into my bathroom!!?"

I just started a sexual relationship with a blind woman, which is rewarding, but very challenging. It took me forever to get the sound of her husband's voice 'just-right'.

My girlfriend's parents are very religious. The first time that I was at their house, her dad told me that we weren't allowed to sleep together, which sucks because he's really fucking sexy!

A mother asks her son, "Why aren't you talking to Mark anymore? You two used to be the closest of friends?" The son replies, "Well, would you like to talk to someone who always acts stupid, uses drugs and dinks booze every day?" The mother says, "Absolutely not!" The son says, "Well, neither would Mark!"

'Trampolines' used to be called 'jumpolines', until your mom jumped on one back in the 70's!

I farted at work the other day. My co-worker tried to open the window, but then second guessed his decision. My fart must have smelled extremely horrible, because we work in a submarine!

I saw this poor old lady fall down the stairs today. At least, I assume that she was poor because she only had five dollars in her wallet!

What is the German name for a virgin? Gutentight!

What's the difference between a hormone and an enzyme? You can't hear an enzyme!

The most effective way to remember your wife's birthday is to forget it once!

How do you describe a blonde surrounded by drooling idiots? Flattered!

What do you call one thousand lawyers at the bottom of the ocean? A good start!

A blonde dyes her hair brown. A few days later, she's driving through the countryside when she stops her car to let a flock of sheep pass. Admiring the cute, wooly animals, she says to the shepherd, "If I can guess how many sheep you have correctly, can I have one?" The shepherd agrees. The blonde thinks for a moment and says, "Three hundred and twelve." The shepherd is amazed, "You're right! Which of the sheep do you want?" The blonde picks the cutest animal. The shepherd says to her, "Okay, how's this for a bet? If I can guess your true hair colour, can I have my dog back?"

What do you get when you cross a Puerto-Rican and an Asian guy? A car thief who can't drive!

Roses are gray, violets are gray, and I am a dog!

Why are there no ice cubes in Poland? They lost the recipe.

If you think that women are the weaker sex, just try pulling the bed sheets back to your side!

What's a man's definition of a romantic evening? Sex!

Why do men die before their wives? Because they want to!

What are three words that women hate to hear while having sex? "Honey, I'm home!"

My wife tried a facial mud mask to make herself more attractive. It worked for a while, but then it fell off!

In his spare time my grandfather races pigeons. I don't know why; he never beats them!

What's the smallest building in Poland? The Polish Hall of Fame!

What do you call and Ethiopian taking a shit? A 'show-off!'

What did the blonde name her zebra? 'Spot!'

I walked into a bar with a friend, and I met a Chinese girl. I asked her for her number, and she said, "Sex! Sex! Sex! Free sex tonight!" I was really excited until my friend told me, "She just said 666-3629."

A major new study determined that humans eat more bananas than monkeys. I can't remember the last time that I ate a monkey.

What's red and smells like blue paint? Red paint!

A doctor tells his patient, "I have good news and bad news. Which do you want to hear first?" The patient says, "The good news." The doctor says, "Your test results came in and you have two days to live." The patient is stunned and then asks, "If that's the good news, what's the bad news?" The doctor replies, "I've been trying to get in contact with you for two days."

How do you make anti-freeze? Take away her blanket!

What do you call a husband who always knows where his wife is? A widower!

If you're choking in a restaurant, you can just say the magic words, "Heimlich Maneuver" and all will be well. The trouble is that it's difficult to say, "Heimlich Maneuver" when you're choking!

Why was the Leper Hockey game cancelled? Because there was a 'face-off' in the corner.

Why did Stevie Wonder fall into the well? Because he couldn't see that well!

I love telling orphans jokes. Who are they going to tell, their parents?

What makes sad people jump? Bridges.

What did one bear say to the other bear? Nothing, bears can't talk!

'I'm sorry' and 'I apologize' mean the same thing, except at a funeral.

What's worse than finding a worm in your apple? The Holocaust!

Little Johnny comes home from school and tells his dad the bad news, "Dad, I got suspended from school again today." His dad asks, "What did you do now?" Little Johnny replies, "Well, I was in math class and the teacher asked me what's 2 times 3, and I said six." Little Jonny's dad says, "Okay..." Then Little Johnny says, "Then she asked me what's 3 times 2." Little Johnny's dad says, "What's the fucking difference?!" Little Johnny says, "That's what I said!"

How did the Pillsbury Dough Boy die? He died of a horrible yeast infection!

A man walks into a library and asks to check out a book on how to commit suicide. The librarian responds, "Fuck off! You won't bring the book back!"

If at first you don't succeed, then skydiving isn't for you!

What's the hardest part about eating a vegetable? The wheelchair!

My grandfather says that I'm too hooked on technology. I got pissed off, and I called him a 'hypocrite' and then unplugged his life support!

My wife told me that she's going to slam my head into the keyboard if I don't get off of the computer. I think that she's just jokinlkyuwhfwdwvhdvefvbvfbfvbefvbewfbcv656278!

The other day my wife asked me to pass her lipstick. I passed her the glue stick by accident. She hasn't spoken to me since!

A man comes home from the pickle factory and tell his wife, "Honey, I have bad news." His wife asks, "What?" He says, "I got fired from work today." She says, "You've been working there for twenty years, what the hell did you do?" The man says, "Nothing much, all that I did was stick my dick in the pickle slicer." His wife says, "Are you crazy? What the fuck is wrong with you? How's your dick?" The man says, "My dick is fine!" She then asks, "How's the pickle slicer?" The man responds, "Oh, she got fired too."

A mom asks her son, "Anton, do you think that I'm a bad mother?" Her son replies, "My name is Paul!!!"

Friends are like bananas. If you peel their skin and eat them, they die.

A doctor tells his patient, "You have cancer and Alzheimer's disease." The patient replies, "Well, at least I don't have cancer!"

What's the difference between a fish and a pig? They both have gills, except for the pig.

I was drinking a Margarita when the waitress screamed, "Does anyone know CPR?" I shouted out, "I know the entire alphabet!" And we all laughed and laughed, except for one guy.

When the Hulk goes off into a vicious rage and destroys everything, he's incredible. But when I do it, I'm an alcoholic!

Fuck me if I'm wrong, but isn't your name Cinderella?

Why did the waiter spit in his customer's soup? Because he's a horrible waiter and he's an asshole.

Why are vegetarians so good at giving blow jobs? Because they're used to eating nuts!

What do a milk jug and a 'make a wish' kid have in common? They both have expiration dates.

What did one tampon say to the other tampon as they walked by each other on the street? Nothing, they were both 'stuck up cunts!'

The lady janitor at my office asked me if I could hang out with her after work and smoke a joint. I told her, "No, I have a hard time dealing with 'high maintenance women!'

I was shocked when I found out that my toaster wasn't waterproof!

Why did Mozart kill all of his chickens? Because, when he asked them who the best composer was, they all said, "Bach, Bach, Bach!"

I started crying when my dad was cutting up onions. 'Onions' was such a good dog!

What do you call a dinosaur that orgasms every time that you rub it? A Clitosauras.

What do Tiger Woods and baby seals have in common? They both get clubbed by Scandinavians.

A patient goes to his doctor to get his test results. The doctor says, "I have good news and I have bad news. Which would you like to hear first?" The patient says, "The bad news." The doctor says, "Well, you have inoperable brain cancer and you're going to die." The patient is floored and then asks, "What the hell is the good news!" The doctor says, "Do you see that really sexy receptionist over there? I fucked her last night!"

My parents raised me as an only child, which really pissed off my brother!

A termite walks into a bar and asks, "Is the bartender here?"

I'll never forget my grandma's last words, "Hey Jimmy, what are you doing in here with that hammer?"

Why is it important to take two pairs of pants when you play golf? In case you get a hole-in-one!

How many cops does it take to throw a black man down a flight of stairs? None! He fell!

What do you call two lesbians in the closet? A liquor cabinet!

How do you wake up Lady Gaga in the morning? Poker face!

A duck is checking out of the corner store and puts a tube of Chapstick on the counter. He then says to the clerk, "Put it on my bill!"

A horse walks into a bar. They bartender says, "Hey!" The horse says, "Sure!"

Did you hear that Michael Jackson and Elton John were working on a duet before Michael Jackson died? The name of the song was 'Don't Let Your Son go Down on Me'.

My girlfriend asked me if I've ever pissed in the shower. I said, "Hasn't everyone?" She said, "What the fuck? That's gross. What's wrong with you?" I replied, "These things happen while you're taking a shit!"

What's the difference between dollars and Jews? I'd give a shit if I lost six million dollars.

Your Momma's so fat that her picture from last Christmas is still printing!

What is black and screams? Stevie Wonder answering the iron!

I run faster horny than you do scared!

I have an epileptic midget neighbour who loves pizza. Every day he has 'Little Seizures'.

A Catholic woman has had six children in five years and is tired of being pregnant. She goes to a priest who advises her to sleep in a chair every night and to put her feet in a ten-gallon bucket of water. The woman is puzzled by this but agrees to follow her priest's instructions. Three months later the woman comes back and tells the priest that she's pregnant again. "Did you do what I had suggested?", asks the priest. "Yes and no," replies the woman. "I put my feet in water, but I couldn't find a ten-gallon bucket, so, I put them in two five-gallon buckets instead."

What's the difference between a Catholic priest and acne? Acne waits until you're older than thirteen to come on your face.

Why did 'Waldo' go to therapy? He wanted to find himself!

I like my girls just like I like my wine, twelve years old and locked in the basement!

Why can't orphans play baseball? They don't know where home is.

What did the redneck say to his girlfriend as they were breaking up? "I sure hope that we can still be brother and sister."

What's the difference between Jesus and a painting of Jesus? It only takes one nail to hang up the painting.

After death, what is the only organ in the female body that remains warm? My penis!

A son tells his father, "Dad, I have an imaginary girlfriend." The father sighs and says, "You know, you could do better." The son says, "Thanks dad." The dad replies, "I wasn't talking to you, I was talking to your imaginary girlfriend."

My wife left me a note on the fridge that said, "This isn't working..." I opened the fridge door and it's working just fine!

A Chinese couple are lying in bed when the husband says to his wife, "I want to try 69." The wife says, "You know that I don't like pea pods and broccori, you rooser!"

There are three types of people in the world. Those who can count, and those that can't.

A pedophile and a little boy are walking into the woods in the dark of night. The little boy says, "I'm scared!" The pedophile says, "You think that you're scared? I have to walk out of this forest all by myself!"

I visited my friend at his new house, and he told me to make myself at home. So, I kicked him out of the house and changed the sheets. I hate having visitors!

What do you call a man who says that he doesn't masturbate? A LIAR!

How did Captain Hook die? Jock itch.

What's the definition of 'frustration'? A midget playing with a Yo-Yo.

A guy asks his buddy to go out for drinks on Saturday night. The buddy replies, "Not tonight man. I got hammered last night and I blew chunks." The guy says, "No worries... puking isn't a big deal. Get your shit together and lets party tonight." The buddy replies, "You don't understand, Chunks is my dog!"

Some mornings, it's just not worth chewing through the leather straps!

Where did Jimmy go after getting lost in a mine field? Everywhere!

A blonde walk into a pet store and asks for a big bag of bird seed. "How many birds have you got?", asks the shopkeeper. "None.", says the blonde. "I was hoping to grow some."

Two pollocks are walking down the street when one says to the other, "Oh, shit! Look at that dead bird!" The other pollock looks up into the sky and says, "Where?"

When your pet bird sees you reading the newspaper, does he wonder why you're sitting there staring at his carpet?

When I was born, my mother had a C-section. Most people have a hard time knowing that, but whenever I leave my house, I go out through the window.

A husband comes home from work and yells up the stairs, "Honey! Pack your bags, I just won the lottery!" She responds, "Should I pack for somewhere warm or cold? The husband says, "I don't give a shit, just get the fuck out!"

What's the difference between Michael Jackson and a shopping bag? One is white, plastic, and dangerous for your kids to play with, and you put groceries in the other!

How many times can 50 fit into 9? Get into my windowless van with carpeted walls and find out!

What's the difference between Jesus and the dead baby that I have in the basement? Jesus died a virgin!

What do you call 12 guys sitting naked on each other's shoulders? A Scrotum Pole!

How is pubic hair like parsley? You push them both to the side before you start eating!

What do you get when you jingle Santa's balls? A white Christmas!

What comes after '69'? Mouthwash!

What did the Mexican say when two houses fell on him? "Get off me, Homes!"

What's a southern gay guy's favorite dessert? Ass cream cones!

A blonde, a brunette and a redhead all escape from prison. While on the run, they hear police sirens, so they decide to hide inside a nearby barn. They see three burlap sacks and they decide to hide inside of them. The police arrive and inspect the barn. An officer sees the sacks. He kicks the brunettes sack and hears, "Meow". He figures that there's a cat in it and then proceeds to kick the second sack. Then he hears, Woof. He thinks that it must be a dog. He then kicks the third sack with the blonde inside of it and she shouts out, "Potatoes!"

How do you sink a submarine full of blondes? Knock on the door!

How many pollacks does it take to play hide-and-seek? Just one.

What do you call a black man flying a plane? A pilot, you racist!

If a four-hundred-pound lawyer and a ninety-pound lawyer both jumped off of the Empire State building at precisely the exact same time, who would hit the ground first? Who the fuck cares!!!

A waiter walks up to a table full of Jewish women and asks, "Is anything okay?"

What do dildos and tofu have in common? They're both meat substitutes.

Did you hear about the cannibal who went on a diet? He only ate midgets!

Hannibal Lecter is seeing someone new, but she hates talking to him while he's nauseous. He keeps bringing up old girlfriends!

How do they practice safe sex in Scotland? They brand the sheep that kick.

Ten blondes and a brunette are on a rock-climbing expedition when some grappling hooks give way leaving them all clinging onto one rope. To prevent any more hooks falling out, they all agree that someone has to let go of the rope to reduce the weight. For an agonizing moment no one volunteers, but then the brunette gives a rousing speech saying that she will sacrifice herself to save the others, and all of the blondes applauded!

How was copper wire invented? Two Scotsmen fighting over a penny!

What do you call a man with no arms, no legs, and no torso? Dick.

"Did you hear about the actress that stabbed herself? Reese... Reese...". "Witherspoon?" "No, with her knife, you dumbass!"

What's the difference between boogers and broccoli? Kids don't eat broccoli!

What's the difference between a dead child molester and a dead rabbit lying at the side of the road? There are skid marks in front of the rabbit.

What is a blind person's favorite colour? Black!

A man is driving down a deserted road. He pulls up to an intersection, and rolls through the stop sign. Out of nowhere, a cop pulls him over. "Do you know why I pulled you over?" asks the cop. "Hey, I slowed down. Didn't I?", asks the man. The cop replies, "You must come to a full stop at the sign."

"Stop, slow down, what the difference" argues the man. "I'll show you," says the cop, who then pulls out his Billy-stick and starts beating the man over the head viciously. "So," he says, "Do you want me to stop, or slow down?"

What's black and sits at the top of the stairs? Stephen Hawking after a house fire!

One time a cop pulled me over for running a stop sign. He said, "Didn't you see the stop sign?" I said, "Yeah, but I don't believe everything that I read!

A husband says to his blonde wife, "I don't believe it! You just backed over my bike!" The wife replies, "Well, you shouldn't have left it on the lawn!"

I've figured out how to avoid parking tickets. I've taken the windshield wipers off of my car!

I had to go next door to watch my neighbour's cat while he was away. Now there's a giant pile of crap and a puddle of pee on his kitchen floor. Hopefully, he'll think that the cat did it!

What do you get when you cross Tina Turner with an orangutan? An ugly orangutan who can sing!

If a white cop had a black dick, he'd beat it to death!

I had an uncle who was a circus clown. When he died, all of his friends went to the funeral in one car!

Four out of five people suffer from diarrhea. So, does that mean that one out of five actually enjoys it?

The Lone Ranger and Tonto are caught in an ambush. The Lone Ranger shouts, "Tonto! There are Indians ahead of us and Indians behind us. And there are Indians on both sides of us! It looks like we're done for!" Tonto looks at the Lone Ranger and says, "What do you mean by 'we', white boy?"

How was break dancing invented? A thief from the ghetto tried to steal the hubcaps off of a moving car!

Why do Italian guys have moustaches? So, they can look 'Justa-like-mama!"

What's 20 inches long and makes a woman scream all night long? Crib death!

What do you call a man with no arms and no legs on the beach? Sandy.

What's the most common allergy in the lesbian population? Nuts!

A girl brings her boyfriend home after a night of drinking. Her parents are home, so she tells him to be quiet. Unfortunately, her boyfriend really needs to use the bathroom. Rather than send him upstairs and risk waking up her parents, she tells him to use the kitchen sink instead. A few minutes later, the boyfriend pokes his head around the corner. His girlfriend whispers, "Have you finished yet?" He says, "Yes! Have you got any toilet paper?"

My grandmother died on her ninetieth birthday. It was a terrible shame; she only opened half of her birthday presents!

A psychiatrist asks his patient, "How long have you believed in reincarnation?" The patient replies, "Ever since I was a baby lobster."

A husband and his wife enter a dentist's office. The husband says to the dentist, "I want a tooth pulled, but I don't want any gas or anesthesia because I'm in a real hurry. Just pull the tooth as quickly as possible." You're a brave man," says the dentist. "Now, which tooth is it?" The husband turns to his wife and says, "Open your mouth and show him which tooth it is, honey."

Did you hear about the pollack who was treated in the emergency room for a concussion and severe head wounds? He tried to commit suicide by hanging himself with a bungee cord.

How can you tell if a blonde has been using the computer? There's White-Out on the screen. How can you tell if two blondes have been using the computer? There's writing on the White-Out!

What do you call a white guy surrounded by ten African Americans? Coach.

What do you call a white guy surrounded by one thousand African Americans? Warden.

A pedophile, a priest, and a homosexual walk into a bar. Then a second guy walks in.

Two peanuts were walking down the street. One was assaulted!

A dyslexic, and an agnostic insomniac stayed up all night wondering if there really was a "Dog."

What do you call two lesbians in a canoe? Fur traders!

A man is working at a lumber yard and accidentally cuts off all of his fingers. He goes straight to the emergency room, where the doctor says, "Give me the fingers, and I'll see what I can do." The man replies, "I don't have the fingers." The doctor says, "What do you mean that you don't have the fingers? We could have done microsurgery; I could have reattached all of them. Why in the world didn't you bring the fingers?" The man replies, "I couldn't pick them up!"

What's the quickest way to get into a blonde's pants? Pick them up off of the floor!

A dog with three legs walks into a saloon. He says, "I'm looking for the man who shot my paw!"

A mailman meets a boy and a huge dog. The mailman asks the boy, "Does your dog bite?" "No," replies the boy, as the dog proceeds to bite the mailman's leg. The mailman screams, "You said that he doesn't bite!" The boy replies, "He's not my dog!"

Did you hear about the Polish coyote? It got stuck in a trap, chewed off three of its legs and it was still stuck!

How can you tell if your dog is kinky? He has sex in the missionary position!

24 hours in a day, 24 beers in a case. Coincidence? I think not!

Why is American beer served cold? So, you can tell the difference between it and piss!

My wife hates the sight of me when I'm drunk. I hate the sight of her when I'm sober!

Rehab is for quitters!

A man asks his dentist, "Can you recommend anything for my yellow teeth?" The dentist responds, "Wear a brown tie!"

Did you hear about the man that put his fake teeth in backwards? He ate himself to death!

I tried going to the Special Olympics, but I couldn't find a parking spot anywhere near the place!

Quasimodo comes home and finds Esmeralda holding a wok and a laundry basket. "Great!" says Quasimodo. "Are you cooking Chinese tonight?" "No," says Esmeralda. "I'm ironing your shirts!"

How can you tell if you have a serious acne problem? Blind people try to read your face!

How does a blind person know if he's close to the ground while skydiving? His dog's leash goes slack.

A friend of mine got her birth control pills mixed up with her Valium. She now has 14 kids, but she doesn't give a shit!

What does DNA stand for? National Dyslexics Association!

When life gives you melons, you might be dyslexic!

I told my girlfriend that she drew her eyebrows on too high. She looked surprised!

A mother asks her son, "Why did you swallow the money that I just gave you?" Her son replies, "You said that it was my lunch money!"

What's the number one cause of divorce? Marriage!

A French explorer, an English explorer and a Canadian explorer are captured by a fierce tribe of Indians. The chief tells them, "We're going to kill you, and then use your hides to build a canoe. In honour of your sacrifice, you may choose your method of death." The Frenchman says, "I'll take dee poison." The chief gives the Frenchman some poison, and he drinks it down and then shouts, "Viva la France!" The Englishman says, "A pistol for me, please." The chief gives him a pistol. The Englishman shouts, "God save the Queen!" and proceeds to blow his brains out. The Canadian says, "Can I have a fork, please?" The chief is puzzled but gives the Canadian a fork anyways. The Canadian takes the fork and starts stabbing himself all over his body. "What are you doing?" shouts the chief. The Canadian says, "So much for your canoe, asshole!"

Why is 'dyslexia' so hard to spell?

A man says to his friend, "I'm really fed up with my dog. He'll chase anyone on a bike." His friend asks him, "What are you going to do? Are you going to put him down?" The man says, "No. I just think that I'll take his bike away!"

What's Polish and dead in a closet? The hide and seek champion from 1995!

What do you call a brunette with bad breath? A blonde standing on her head!

My teachers told me that I'd never amount to anything because I procrastinate too much. I told them, "Just you wait!"

A Christian friend of mine said that sex between two men is wrong in their eyes. I said, "You're right! They're supposed to have sex in the butt!"

Why did everyone like the mushroom so much? Because he was a fungi!

What do you call a Mexican with a rubber toe? Roberto!

What's the difference between hungry and horny? Where you stick the cucumber!

A doctor visits his patient lying in a hospital bed. "I'm sorry," says the doctor, "but I have good news and bad news." "Don't hold back," says the man, "Tell me the bad news." The doctor replies, "Your condition was worse than we thought. We had to amputate both of your legs." The man is shocked and then asks, "What the hell is the good news?" The doctor replies, "The man in the bed next to you wants to buy your slippers."

Our whole family is very concerned about my grandfather's Viagra addiction. Especially Grandma, she's taking it really hard.

Did you know that they took the word 'gullible' out of the dictionary?

What's better than roses on your piano? Tulips on your organ.

How do you find a fat girls vagina? Dip her in flour and look for the wet spot.

What do you call a short black person? By their name, you racist!

What do you call a rapper with Parkinson's disease? A chocolate shake!

What's the difference between Usain Bolt and Hitler? Usain Bolt can finish a race!

A blind man grabs his eye seeing dog by the tail and starts spinning him around above his head in the pet store. A concerned onlooker asks him, "What the hell are you doing?" The blind man says, "I'm just taking a look around!"

Have you ever kissed a bunny rabbit between the ears? (Pull out both of your front pant pockets and ask, "Would you like to?")

Knock, knock. Who's there? May I come in? May I come in who? May I come in you?

My wife asked me where I would like to be buried. Apparently, 'Balls deep in your sister', wasn't the correct answer!

How much semen does a gay guy have? A butt load!

What do you call the lesbian version of a cock block? A beaver dam!

My dad always warned me about anal sex. He would always say, "Son, this might hurt a bit."

Why do sumo wrestlers shave their legs? Because they don't want to be confused with feminists.

What do tightrope walking and getting a blow job from Grandma have in common? Whatever you do, DON'T LOOK DOWN!

A woman just asked me if I liked thighs or breasts. I told her that I liked shaved pussies and anal sex. Apparently, this is an inappropriate response to the cashier at KFC!

The judge asks the child molester, "How does five to ten years sound?" The child molester then rubs his hands together intensely and says, "SEXY!!!!"

My girlfriend is 19 years old and I'm 29 years old. We went out to eat at a restaurant last night and the whole time I had to deal with people calling me a 'disgusting cradle robber'. It totally ruined our ten-year anniversary.

Did you hear about the new German microwave? It seats twenty-five!

Where do you send Jewish kids with A.D.D.? Concentration camp!

I just found out that I'm colorblind. My diagnosis came completely out of the 'Purple!'

I want to die peacefully in my sleep like my grandfather, not screaming and yelling like the passengers in his car!

Did you know that diarrhea is hereditary? It's because it runs in your genes!

My girlfriend is always stealing my T-shirts and sweatshirts, which pisses me off. But if I wear her dress, then suddenly, "WE NEED TO TALK!"

What do you call a black man with oversized kneecaps? Knee-grow!

A math teacher asks, "If I have five bottles in one hand and six bottles in the other, what do I have? Little Johnny answers, "A drinking problem!"

Before I criticize a man, I like to walk a mile in his shoes. That way, when I do criticize him, I'm a mile away and I have his shoes!

Today a man knocked on my door and asked me for a small donation towards the local swimming pool, so, I gave him a small plastic cup full of water!

I think that my neighbour is stalking me! She has been Googling my name on her computer non-stop. I saw it through my telescope last night!

What has four legs and flies? A dead raccoon!

Why did Kamikaze pilots wear helmets?

You know that you're a narcissist when you scream out your own name during an orgasm!

It's the middle of the night and a couple are sleeping in bed when there's a knock at the door. The man goes downstairs in his nightrobe to answer the door. There is a drunk on his doorstep. The drunk asks the man, "Can you give me a push?" The man says, "No! Do you know what time it is?!" The man slams the door shut and goes back upstairs and tells to his wife what had just happened. "You should be ashamed of yourself," says the wife. "That man was asking for your help, and you turned him down! I don't care if he was drunk. Go outside and help the man push his car!" The man gives in, puts on some clothes, and goes outside to find the drunk. He opens his front door, and shouts out, "Hey, do you still want a push?" The drunk shouts back, "Yeah! I'm over here on your swing!"

If corn oil is made from corn, and vegetable oil is made from vegetables, what is baby oil made from?

I was cuddling in bed with my girlfriend the other day when I said to her, "I'm the luckiest guy on the planet". My transvestite girlfriend replied, "Me too!"

Which idiot decided to put braille dots on the keypad at a drive-up ATM?

Should crematoriums give discounts to burn victims?

What's worse than finding a maggot in the apple that you just bit into? Finding half of a maggot.

A doctor prescribes testosterone to a woman to treat her mild hormonal imbalance. Two weeks later she returns to her doctor for a follow-up. She says, "Doctor, since you put me on those pills, I've noticed some extra hair growth." "Well, that's one of the side effects," says the doctor. "It's nothing to worry about. Where have you noticed this hair?" The woman replies, "ON MY BALLS!"

Confucius say: "Avoid cutting yourself while slicing vegetables by getting someone else to hold them."

How do you avoid arguments with your wife about lifting up the toilet seat? Just piss in the sink!

Before you attempt to remove a stubborn stain from an article of clothing, circle it with permanent marker. That way when you remove the clothing from the washing machine, you can quickly check to see if the stain is gone.

How do you know if a letter is from a leper? His tongue is still in the envelope.

How many gay men does it take to screw in a light bulb? Just one, but it takes a whole emergency room to get it out again!

My brother-in-law just died. He was a karate expert who joined the army. The first time that he saluted his superior officer, he killed himself.

How do you know if a gay man has robbed your house? Your house had been re-decorated, there are flowers in the bathroom, and he's still hiding in your closet!

A psychologist asks his patient, "What does this inkblot look like?" The patient responds, "It looks like a horrible, ugly blob of pure evil, that sucks the souls out of men into a vortex of sin and degradation." The doctor replies, "Um, the inkblot is over there. You're looking at a photo of my wife!"

"Mommy, mommy! What's a nymphomaniac?" "Shut up and help me get grandma off of the doorknob."

You know that you're a redneck when your wife weighs more than your refrigerator.

What do you have if you've got two really big green balls in your fists? The Joly Green Giant's undivided attention.

I tried some of that aphrodisiac rhino horn. Now I have an undesirable urge to charge madly at Land Rovers!

What has two thumbs and loves getting blow jobs? Point your thumbs towards yourself and say, "Thissss guyyyy!"'

Why do Scotsmen wear rubber boots? To put the sheep's back legs in them to keep them from escaping.

Confucius say, "Man who jizzes into cash register come into money.

Once I've used up all of my sick days, I'm going to call in dead.

A teacher walks into her classroom and announces to the class that on each Friday, she will ask a question to the class and anyone who answers the answer correctly will be allowed to miss school on Monday. On the first Friday, the teacher asks, "How many grains of sand are on the beach?" None of the students knew the answer. The following Friday, the teacher asks, "How many stars are in the sky?" Again, no one knew the answer. Little Johnny is determined to have a three-day weekend. Getting ready for the next Friday, Little Johnny takes two ping pong balls and paints them black. The next day he takes them to school in a paper bag. At the end of the day, just when the teacher says, "Here's this week's question," Little Johnny empties the paper bag and sends the black ping pong balls rolling to the front of the classroom. The kids in the class all start laughing. The teacher says, "Okay, who's the comedian with the black balls?" Little Johnny stands up immediately and says, "Chris Rock! See you next Tuesday!"

If life gives you lemons, squeeze the juice into a water gun and shoot other people in the eyes!

Confucius say, "Never get behind someone wearing a ski mask in a line at the bank."

What do your mother-in-law and a slinky have in common? They're both fun to watch tumble down the stairs.

You know that you're a narcissist when you scream out your own name during an orgasm!

A chubby woman goes to her doctor for a physical examination. She's asked to take off her clothes and says, "I'm ashamed, doctor. I guess I let myself go." The doctor says, "You don't look that bad." He then holds a tongue depressor on her tongue and says, "Open your mouth and say moo!"

Why is there a light in the fridge, and not in the freezer?

Dr. Dave was extremely upset with himself because he had sex with one of his patients. He was especially upset because he's a veterinarian.

"Mommy, mommy! Can I wear a bra now that I'm sixteen?" "Shut up, Albert!"

You're about as useful as an ashtray on a motorcycle.

What do you get when you cross an elephant and a rhino? 'Hell if I know!'

They say that opposites attract. I hope that you find and intelligent, and good-looking partner who doesn't smell like shit!

A nurse in an insane asylum is making her rounds and she sees Jerry in his room pretending to drive a car. "I'm going to Cleveland," he tells her. Later that day, the nurse comes by again and sees Jerry pretending to park his car. "I'm in Cleveland!", he says. The nurse then checks in on Jerry's neighbour, Frank. She sees Frank masturbating frantically. She says, "Frank, what the hell are you doing?" Frank replies, "I'm fucking Jerry's wife while he's out of town!"

"Mommy, mommy! What's a werewolf?" "Be quiet and go comb your face!"

"I don't like country music, but I don't mean to denigrate those who do. And for those people who like country music, denigrate means 'put down.''

Which is better, an electric guitar or a harmonica? The electric guitar. You can't beat a harmonica player to death with a harmonica.

What do you call a man with no arms and no legs under a car? Jack.

Why are Peurto-Ricans so good at break dancing? Because of all of the clothes hangers that they had to dodge while in the womb!

How do you have sex with a fat girl? Slap her leg and ride the wave in!

Your momma is so ugly that she made 'One Direction' go the other way!

What's the first thing that they teach soldiers in the French army? To raise their arms in the air to surrender.

Confucius say: "A mousetrap placed on top of your alarm clock prevent you from going back to sleep."

My psychiatrist gave me a chocolate easter bunny and I ate it. He said, "Had you eaten the ears first, you would have been normal. Had you eaten the feet first, you would have an inferiority complex. Had you eaten the tail first you would have latent homosexual tendencies, and had you eaten the breasts first you would have a latent oedipal complex." I said, "What does it mean when you bite out the eyes and scream, 'Stop staring at me!'? The doctor said, "It means that you have a tendency towards self-destruction." I asked, "Well, what do you recommend?" The doctor said, "Go for it!"

Why is it called Alcoholics Anonymous when the first thing that you do is stand up and say, "Hi, my name is Bobby, and I'm an alcoholic."

What do you call a terrorist with a wooden leg? Shit on a stick. What do you call a terrorist with two wooden legs? A waste of wood.

You remind me of the ocean. You make me sick!

How do you blindfold a Chinaman? With dental floss!

A friend tells his buddy, "I've got a great knock, knock joke for you. You start." His buddy says, "Knock, knock." The friend then asks, "Who's there?" (Then silence)

What was the title of Michael Jackson's final book that he was working on? 'The Ins and Outs of Child Rearing".

A girlfriend asks her boyfriend, "How could you sleep with her?" The boyfriend responds, "Umm, she's hot." The girlfriend asks, "Didn't you think about me in all of this?" The boyfriend answers, "I thought about you the whole time so I wouldn't blow my load early!"

What is the national bird of Italy? The fly!

What are the pluses about having Alzheimer's disease? You can buy and wrap your own presents, and you are constantly making new friends!

Your acne is so bad that you look like the goalie for the local dart team!

When my boss asked me who was the stupid one, me or him, I told him that everybody knows that he doesn't hire stupid people!

"Thanks for explaining the word, 'many' to me. It means a lot!"

Why do brides wear white? Because it's important that the dishwasher matches the fridge and the stove!

Say what you want about pedophiles, but at least they drive slow through school zones.

What do you get when you cross an apple with a nun? A computer that won't go down!

I bought a self-learning language record to learn German. I turned it on and went to sleep. During the night, the record skipped. The next day I could only stutter in German.

Two drunks are sitting in a bar when one of them throws up all over himself. The puker says, "Damn, my wife is going to kill me when she sees this." The second drunk says, "No problem. Just put twenty dollars in your shirt pocket. When your wife asks what it's for, say that a drunk man threw up on you at the bar and he gave you twenty dollars for dry cleaning." "That's a great idea," says the first drunk, and they both get hammered until closing. Later, the drunk with puke on him returns home. His wife sees him and freaks out. She says, "Look at you! You're covered in vomit!" "It's not my fault," says the husband. "A man threw up on me and then he gave me twenty dollars for dry cleaning," He then hands her the bills that he had. His wife counts the money and says, "There's forty dollars here!" The husband replies, "Oops. I forgot to tell you, he shit in my pants too!"

A masked man rushes into a bank and points a banana at the cashier. "This is a fuck-up!", he shouts. The cashier asks the robber, "Don't you mean a hold-up?". "No," says the man. "It's a fuck-up. I left my gun on the bus."

When you go into a trial in court you are putting your life in the hands of twelve people who weren't smart enough to get out of jury duty.

In court, a prosecutor asks the witness, "Is it true, that on September 3rd you and the accused both visited a brothel dressed as nuns and both of you asked to be whipped senseless by a nude midget?" The witness says, "I'm not sure. What date was that again?"

How do you make a blonde's eyes sparkle? Shine a flashlight into her ear!

Your momma is so fat that she has little momma's orbiting around her!

What's the difference between a Mexican and a park bench? A park bench can support a family of four.

I asked my wife to let me know the next time that she has an orgasm. She told me that she doesn't like to bother me while I'm at work!

I saw my wife putting on her 'sexy' underwear this morning. That can only mean one thing, it's laundry day!

My wife and I have agreed to never go to bed angry with each other. So far, we've been up for three days!

A wife asks her husband, "Ready for dinner honey?" He asks her, "What are my choices?" The wife responds, "Yes, or no!"

Why did more black guys die in Vietnam than white guys? Every time that the heard. "Get down!", they jumped up and started dancing!

What did the Puerto-Rican family sell at their garage sale? "MY STUFF!"

What do you call a girl with one leg? 'Eileen.' What do you call a Chinese girl with one leg? 'Irene!'

How do Chinese people name their kids? They throw their silverware down the stairs, "Ting ding dang ding, wong'. Why do Chinese people use chopsticks? Because all of their silverware is in the basement!

Why did Frosty the Snowman pull down his pants? Because the snow blower was in the driveway!

A woman walks up to a wrinkly old man sitting on a park bench. "You look very content," she says. "What's your secret to a long, happy life?" The man replies, "I smoke sixty cigarettes a day, I drink a case of beer every day, I eat nothing, but fatty meat and I never exercise." "That's amazing!", says the woman. "Just how old are you?", she asks. The man replies, "Twenty-six."

What's the definition of impossible? Trying to slam a revolving door.

How do you make a hormone? Don't pay her.

A man who really needed to shit proclaimed, "I need to free Nelson Mandela!"

You know that you're a redneck when your wife has a beer belly, and you find it attractive.

No one has ever complained about a parachute not opening.

I quit smoking. I feel better. I smell better. And it's safer to drink out of the old beer cans lying around the house!

How did the Polish hockey team die? They drowned during spring training!

I could tell that my parents hated me. My bath toys were a toaster and a radio!

A Pollack walks into his house with a dog turd in his hand. He shows it to his wife and says, "Look at what I almost stepped in!"

My uncle went to see a mime show and had a seizure. He was tossed out of the theater because they thought he was heckling.

Never moon a werewolf.

Three guys, an American, a Canadian and a Pollack are interviewing for a job in the secret service. The interviewer says to the three, "Here is a loaded gun for each one of you. On the other side of those three doors are your wives. You're all instructed to go through your individual door and kill your wife on the other side. The American goes in first and immediately comes out and says, "I can't do it! She's the mother of my children." They tell him that his loyalty to his wife has earned him a solid consideration for the job. Then the Canadian goes in. He comes right back out and says, "I can't live without my wife. We always watch the hockey game together, and we do it doggystyle so we both can watch at the same time!" He's told by the interviewers that they admire his frankness. Then the Polack goes in. Immediately six shots ring out in succession, and then there are sounds of a struggle and screaming, and then silence. The Pollack then storms out of the door and says, "You idiots, that gun was loaded with blanks. I had strangle the bitch!"

Your Momma's so ugly that she practices birth control by leaving the lights on.

What did the leper say to the hooker? "Keep the tip!"

How do you spot a blind man in a nudist colony? It's not hard!

What's black and white and read all over? A newspaper!

My son asked me what it was like to be married? I screamed at him, "Leave me alone!" And then, when he did, I shouted at him, "Why are you ignoring me?!"

What's black and white and red all over? A nun rolling down a rocky hill!

Why was six afraid of seven? Because seven ate nine and nine is a mirror image of six doing a headstand!

Why was six afraid of seven? Because seven was a registered six offender!

How many times does a baby have to spin around in the microwave before it explodes? I'm not sure, I was too busy jerking off!

Why are Mike Tyson's eyes red after sex? From the mace!

A man and a woman are sitting at the bar and start talking. The woman says that she was just had been recently divorced. She said that her husband left her because he thought that she was too 'kinky'. The man replies, "My wife divorced me for the same reason!" They have a couple of more drinks and decide to go back to her place. Once they're there, she says, "Let me go into the bedroom to get into something more comfortable." She's in the bedroom for a while and then comes out wearing a leather outfit with holes for the nipples, a leather hat, stiletto heels, a choke chain, and a whip. She then says to the guy, "Okay, let's get kinky." He blurts out, "I just fucked your dog and shit in your purse! I'm outta here!"

What do you call Mike Tyson with no arms and no legs? "Pussy, pussy, pussy!"

What's yellow and green and eats nuts? Gonorrhea!

What has thirty thousand feet and still can't walk? "Jerry's Kids!"

How do you kill 200 flies at once? Hit an Ethiopian in the face with a frying pan!

What comes from outer space and has three balls? 'E.T.', Extra Testicle!

Why don't witches wear underwear? So, they can get a better grip on the broom!

What's the hardest part about being a pedophile? Trying to fit in.

I need to develop some patience, IMMEDIATELY!

When your wife gets upset, just remember that saying a simple, "Calm down" in a soothing voice is all that it takes to get her more upset!

Two fish are in a tank. One turns to the other and says, "You man the guns, and I'll drive!"

What's the worst thing about being Grandpa? Having to have sex with Grandma!

Jeff walks into a bar and sees his friend Paul slumped over at the bar. He walks over to ask Paul, "What's wrong?" Paul replies, "Well, you know that gorgeous girl at work that I want to ask out?" Jeff replies, "I sure do." Paul says, "Every time that I see her, I get a hard-on." Jeff chuckles at this. Paul says, "Well, I finally mustered up the courage to ask her out and she said 'yes'." Paul said that he was so worried about getting a boner on the date that he duct-taped his cock to his leg so she wouldn't notice. Jeff said, "That's a pretty smart move." Then Paul says, "I get to her front door, and she shows up in the tiniest and sexiest dress that I've ever seen." Jeff asks, "What happened then?" Paul says, "I kicked her in the fucking face!"

Johnny spent many years trying to find a cure for his chronic halitosis and acne only to find that people didn't like him anyway.

A blonde walks into a library and says, "Can I have a burger with fries?" The librarian says, "I'm sorry Miss, but this is a library." The blonde then leans over and whispers quietly to the librarian, "Can I have a burger with fries?"

What's the best thing about being 103 years old? There's no peer pressure!

Knock, knock. Who's there? Spell. Spell who? W.H.O.

What do call someone who kills a gay Mexican? A murderer, you racist homophobe!

What do you tell a woman with two black eyes? "I'm worried that you may be in an abusive relationship and that you should probably seek professional help."

Know-it-alls think that they know everything, except for how fucking annoying they are!

Yesterday, I was riding the escalator at the shopping mall, and I tripped. I fell down those goddamned stairs for an hour and a half before I hit the bottom!

When your wife gets upset, just remember that saying a simple, "Calm down" in a soothing voice is all that it takes to get her more upset!

A husband says to his friend, "I haven't talked to my wife in 18 months." His friend asks, "Why not?" The husband says, "It's because that I don't want to interrupt her!"

I had the courage to come out of the closet and finally admit to my dad that I was gay. Then, when I asked my dad if I could go ice skating on the lake, he answered, "Wait until it gets warmer."

I dated a girl who was so ugly that she was known as a 'Double-Bagger". One brown paper bag for her head, and a brown paper bag for my head in case hers fell off!

A man returns home from work after being on the night shift and goes straight to his bedroom. He sees his wife asleep under the sheets. He decides to take advantage of the situation, and he proceeds to make passionate love to her. After he finishes his sexual encounter, he gets hungry and goes downstairs to get something to eat. He finds his wife in the kitchen with breakfast ready and a hot cup of coffee waiting for him. He asks her, "How did you get down here so fast, we were just making love?" His wife says, "Oh my god, my mother is in the bedroom. She came over complaining of a headache, so I told her to go to our bedroom to get some rest!" Rushing upstairs, the wife goes into the bedroom and asks her mother, "How could you let this happen?!" The mother responds, "I haven't talked to that asshole in years, and I'm not going to start talking to him now!"

Why did the Irishman come home drunk and leave his clothes on the floor? Because he was in them!

Knock, knock. Who's there? Oink, oink. Oink, oink who? Are you a pig or an owl?

Two rednecks are walking down the road when they see a dog licking himself. The one redneck says to his buddy, "Man, I wish that I could do that!" The other redneck says, "Go ahead and try! But he'll probably bite you!"

A grasshopper walks into a bar and the bartender says, "Hey buddy, we have a drink named after you!" The grasshopper replies, "Really? You have a drink named Greg?"

Chris Farley once said, "Be very careful with what you say! I ate the last person that told me a fat joke!"

You're so ugly that I had to quit drinking, just in case I started seeing two of you!

I discovered my wife in bed with another man and I was crushed! I said, "Get off of me, you two fat fucks!"

A Saudi Arabian Prince recently requested that the naked statues in Rome be covered up during his visit. Apparently, his 9-year-old wife found them offensive!

I was pulled over by a policeman and he asked me if I used narcotics. Apparently, 'Usually' was not the right answer!

How do you find out the population of Ethiopia? Roll a cookie down the main street!

A patient wakes up from surgery to see his surgeon standing over him. The surgeon says, "I have good news and bad news. Which do you want to hear first?" The patient says, "The bad news." The surgeon says, "Unfortunately, we amputated the wrong leg." The patient then asks, "What the hell is the good news?" The surgeon replies, "The good news is that your infected leg that we were going to initially amputate is going to be okay!"

Why did the blonde sell her car? To get gas money!

I used to date a midget woman. I was nuts over her!

Jesus walks into a hotel and places a handful of nails on the reception desk. He says to the clerk, "Can you put me up for the night?"

Apparently, I have 'boundary issues.' At least that's what it said in my neighbour's diary!

Why did the Jew soundproof his house? So, his kids couldn't hear the ice cream truck!

What do little boys and drivers with a heavy foot on their brake have in common? They both get 'rear-ended' by Michael Jackson.

Can you use the word, 'herpes' as a Mexican? "I ate my last piece of chicken, but you can have 'herpes'!"

What's better than having sex with a twelve-year-old Vietnamese boy? Nothing!!

What do you get when you mix sheep and semen? Banned from the petting zoo.

What does Michael Jackson like best about 28-year-olds? There's 20 of them!

Why did the monkey fall out of the tree? Because he was dead!

What's the best part of an Alzheimer's disease easter egg hunt? The contestants get to hide their own easter eggs!

A plane carrying an old priest, a hippie and Elon Musk is about to crash and there are only two parachutes for the three passengers. Elon Musk stands up and says, "I'm the world's smartest man. The world would suffer without me." He grabs a pack and jumps out of the plane. The priest then looks at the hippie and says, "Son, I have lived a long and happy life. You have your whole life ahead of you. I think that it's only right that you take the last parachute." The hippie says, "Father, I don't think that we have a problem here. The world's smartest man just grabbed my backpack and jumped out of the plane!"

When you were a kid, you were so ugly that your momma had to tie a pork chop around your neck just to get the dog to play with you.

Confucius say, "Never hit a man with glasses, use your fist."

How many feminists does it take to change a lightbulb? "That's not funny!!!"

How many policemen does it take to screw in a lightbulb? None! They just beat the room for being black!

What do deaf gynecologists do? They read lips!

What do you do when your wife comes out of the kitchen? Shorten the chain!

Who was the most famous Jewish cook? Hitler.

I love to go down to the schoolyard and watch all the children jumping up and down and running around yelling and screaming. They don't know that I'm only using blanks!

How do your stop a lawyer from drowning? Take your foot off of his head!

What's the fastest thing in the world? An Ethiopian chicken, or an Ethiopian with a McDonald's coupon!

A bunch of college guys are driving though an Indian reservation on their way to the cottage for a weekend of fun. Suddenly, their car breaks down and they find themselves stranded at the side of the road. With no cell phone reception on the reservation, the boys are concerned. They open up the hood of the car and see that a piston has broken through the engine wall. All of a sudden, a pick-up truck full of Indians pulls up alongside them when one of the Indians asks them, "What's wrong with your car?" The boy's say, "Piston broke." The Indian says to the guys, "Same here, jump in and let's go for a ride!"

What do you do when an epileptic has an attack in your bathtub? Throw in your soap and laundry!

What's the difference between a blonde and a chest freezer? A chest freezer doesn't fart when you pull your meat out of it!

What do you get when you cross a Pollack and an ape? A retarded ape!

Why are there no Mexicans on Star Trek? Because they don't work in the future either!

What do East Indians get for Halloween? Ghandi!

How do you stop a kid with an afro from jumping on the bed? Put Velcro on the ceiling.

Why do Jamaicans have holes in their upper lips? So that they can see when they whistle!

What do you call a Puerto-Rican on a bike? Thief!

What do you call milkman in high heels? 'Dairy Queen!'

A guy sees a sign outside of a house that says, 'TALKING DOG FOR SALE'. Intrigued, the guy walks up to the door and rings the doorbell. The owner answers the door with the dog by his side. The guy asks the dog, "So what have you done with your life?" The dog answers, "I've led a very full life. I lived in the alps rescuing avalanche victims. Then I served my country in Iraq. Now I spend my days reading to residents at a retirement home." The guy is blown away. He asks the owner, "Why in the world would you want to get rid of an incredible dog like this?" The owner replies, "Because he's a fucking liar. He never did any of that!"

Why are there no Jewish boy scouts? Because their parents refuse to send them to camp!

Did you hear about the cannibal who passed his mother-in-law in the jungle? He forgot to wipe his ass!

What's the definition of mixed emotions? Seeing your mother-in-law back off a cliff in your new car!

What do you call four Mexicans in quicksand? Cuatro-Cinco!

What do you get when you cross a Puerto-Rican and an Asian woman? A car thief who can't drive!

Why were there only six-hundred Mexicans at the Alamo? They only had two cars!

What did the snail say while he was riding on the turtles back? "Wheeee!!"

What's the difference between Martin Luther King Jr. Day and Saint Patrick's Day? On Saint Patrick's Day everybody wants to be Irish.

Mexican jokes and black jokes are pretty much the same. Once you've heard Juan, you've heard Jamal.

How do you keep a blonde busy all day? Write, "Please turn over" on both sides of a piece of paper!

What did Cinderella say when she got to the ball? "ARRRRGHHHH!!".

What do you call ten thousand guys with afros buried up to their foreheads in a field? Afro-turf!

A doctor tells his patient, "You have Ed Zachary Disease." The Patient asks, "What's that?" The doctor tells him, "It's when your face looks Ed Zachary like your ass!"

My friend thinks that he's smart. He told me that onions are the only food that make you cry. After disagreeing with his statement, I threw a coconut at his face!

You're so ugly that the last time that you got a piece of ass was when your fingers punctured the toilet paper!

How do you get five hundred old cows into a barn? Hang up a 'Bingo' sign!

Why do Italian's wear gold chains? So, they know where to stop shaving!

I bought myself a parrot, but it did not say, "I'm hungry", so it died.

Is a hippopotamus a hippopotamus, or is it a really cool opotamus?

A severed foot is the ultimate stocking stuffer!

If you had a friend who was a tightrope walker, and you were walking on the sidewalk with him and he fell, that would be completely UNACCEPTABLE!

I'm a heroine addict... I have to have sex with women who save people's lives!

When I was on acid I would see crazy things, like beams of light. And I would also hear sounds that sounded an awful lot like car horns!

Roses are red, violets are red, shrubs are red, trees are red. Holy shit! My garden is on fire!

How many feminists does it take to change a lightbulb? Two, one to change the lightbulb and the other one to suck on my dick!

What do you hear every time that you see a Puerto-Rican in a three-piece suit? "Will the defendant please rise?"

What would happen if you threw two-hundred dinner plates off of your roof? Nothing, no one is stupid enough to do that and besides, what homeowner would own two-hundred dinner plates?

What's worse than ants in your pants? Uncles!

What's brown and rhymes with Snoop? Dr. Dre!

A black boy walks into the kitchen where his mother is baking. The mother accidentally spills a bag of flour on the boy's head. He looks at his mother and says, Look mama, I'm a white boy!" The boy's mother smacks the boy and says, "Go tell your daddy what you just said!" The boy finds his father and says, "Look daddy, I'm a white boy!" His dad bends the boy over his knee and spanks him. The father then stands the boy back up and asks him, "Now, what do you have to say for yourself?" The boy replies, "I've only been a white boy for five minutes and I already hate you black people!"

A woman told me that I was the biggest that she's ever had. Apparently, "Ditto" wasn't the best response!

What do you do when you miss your ex-wife? Adjust the sights on your rifle!

I would never be caught dead with a necrophiliac, unless he was having sex with my corpse.

A wealthy couple had planned to go out for the evening. The wife decided to give her Butler, 'Jeeves', the night off. She told him that they would be home very late and that he should just enjoy his evening. At the party, the wife wasn't having a good time, so she decided to go home early. Her husband had several important clients there, so he had to stay. When the wife got home, she saw Jeeves sitting in the dining room by himself. She told him to follow her and led him into her room. While in her room, she told Jeeves, "Take off my dress." He carefully took of her dress. She then said, "Jeeves, take off my stockings and garters." He did what she asked. She then asked, "Jeeves, take of my bra and panties." He did as she asked, standing there completely naked. Then she shouts, "Jeeves, if I ever catch you wearing my clothes again, you're fired!"

What do you call a Mexican hooker with no arms or legs? Consuelo!

Pedophiles are fucking immature assholes!

What did one raccoon say to the other raccoon? "Does my breath smell like garbage?"

A guy asks, "What mouse walks on two feet?" His friend replies, "Mickey Mouse?" His friend says, "Yes!", and then asks, "What duck walks on two feet?" His friend says, "Donald Duck". To which the guy replies, "NOOOOO, ALL DUCKS WALK ON TWO FEET!"

What's orange and sounds like a parrot? A carrot!

I couldn't find my potato peeler, so I asked my kids if they've seen it. Apparently, she left me two days ago!

What did the Boston fish market employee say to the magician? "Pick a cod, any cod!"

How do you confuse a blonde? Paint yourself green and throw forks at her!

What's the difference between a rooster and a hooker? A rooster says, "Cock-a-doodle-doo!" A hooker says, "Any-cock-'ll-do!"

I can't help the fact that I like to sleep naked. I wish that the flight attendant could have been more understanding!

What's the difference between Jesus and a whore? The face that they make when you're nailing them!

I hate it when people say that age is only a number! 'Age' is actually a word.

What do you throw a drowning Ethiopian? A Cheerio!

Someone complimented me on my parking today. They left a sweet note on my windshield that said, "Parking Fine."

A policeman says to a suspect, "I'm arresting you for downloading the entire Wikipedia!" The suspect replies, "Wait, I can explain everything!"

Why don't people play UNO with Mexicans? Because they steal all of the green cards!

Why do native American Indians have high cheek bones? Because they're always waiting for the liquor store to open! (Sitting with their elbows on their knees and their hands on their cheeks!)

Why do you push harder on the TV remote when you know the battery is dead?

I like to write jokes. I sit in my hotel at night, and I try to think of something that's funny and then I go to get a pen to write it down. Or, if I'm on the couch and the pen's too far away, I have to convince myself that the joke's not funny.

They say that Flintstones Vitamins are chewable. ALL vitamins are chewable, they just taste shitty!

I'd like to say to the handicapped guy who stole my wallet, "You can hide, but you can't run!"

How do you think the unthinkable? Mike Tyson answers, "With an ithberg!" (Titanic reference.)

What did Kermit the frog say at Jim Henson's funeral? Nothing!

Where did the pirate get his hook? At the second-hand store!

In my free time I like to help blind people. In this case, 'blind' is a verb, not an adjective!

I was sitting on the porch with my wife when I blurted out, "I love you!" She asked, "Is that you or the beer talking?" I said to her, "It's me, talking to my beer!"

I wonder what my parents did to fight off boredom before the internet. I asked my 18 siblings, and they don't know either!

Yesterday I was washing the car with my son. He said, "Dad, can't you wash the car with a sponge instead of me!?"

A white guy in a public restroom noticed the length of the black man's penis who was using the urinal next to him. He said, "I sure wish that I had a cock as impressive as yours." The black man replied, "You can, just tie a string to your cock with a five-pound weight at the other end. Hide it in your pants and you can have a cock like mine." The white guy thanked the black man for the suggestion and went home. A few weeks later, they bumped into each other again. The black man asked, "How's your penis project going?" The white guy replies, "It's going great, I'm halfway there!" "That's great, is you cock getting any longer?" The white guy replies, "No, but it's turning black!"

What do call cheese that's not yours? Nacho cheese!

I love telling dad jokes. Sometimes he even laughs!

What do you call an overweight Chinese psychic? A four-chin-teller!

I hate dad jokes. It's how 'EYE ROLL!'

Midgets and dwarves have 'very little' in common.

My therapist called me 'vengeful'. We'll have to see about that!

What do near-sighted gynecologists and puppies have in common? They both have wet noses!

What do a rhinoceros and a tomato have in common? Neither of them can ride a bike.

A girl phoned me the other day and said, "Come on over to my house, there's nobody home." So, I went to her house and there was nobody there."

What do you call an epileptic having a fit in a lettuce patch? Seizure salad!

I saved a very sexy girl from being attacked last night…I controlled myself!

My psychiatrist told me that I was crazy. I said that that I wanted a second opinion. He said, "Okay, you're fat and ugly too!"

My uncle's dying wish was that he wanted me on his lap when he died. I kind of lost my respect for him because he was sitting in the electric chair when he died.

My wife and I were happy for 20 years. Then we met!

How does Helen Keller smell? Pretty bad, because she's dead!

Did you hear about the Polish carpool? They meet at work in the morning!

A guy meets a "Tinder" date at a carnival. He says to her, "There are so many games! What do you want to do first?" She responds shyly, "I want to get weighed!" They both go to the "Guess your weight" booth and she wins a stuffed zebra. He asks, "What next?" She looks directly into his eyes and says, "I want to get weighed!" So, they return to the "Guess your weight" booth and this time she doesn't win anything. The vendor had a good memory. The guy, annoyed by the date so far, asks, "Now what?" She looks right into his face and says in a firm tone, "I-WANT-TO-GET-WEIGHED!" He ends the date right there and then and he storms off. Dejected, the girl goes home to her roommate who asks, "How did your date go?" The girl throws her stuffed zebra to the ground and says, "It was wousy!"

My girlfriend left me because apparently, I never listen. She could have had the courtesy to tell me that!

What do you get when you mix human DNA and whale DNA? Banned from SeaWorld!

They wouldn't let me join the KKK because my blood line wasn't pure enough. It turns out that my parents weren't even related!

Apparently, the hornier that you are, the more forgetful that you are. Oh, by the way, did you know that the hornier that you are, the more forgetful that you are?

I went to the store to buy camouflage pants the other day, but for the life of me, I couldn't find any!

If the earth was flat, cats would push everything off of it!

What's the difference between a pizza and a Jew? A pizza doesn't scream when you put it in the oven!

How does a woman scare a gynecologist? By becoming a ventriloquist.

Whoever said the phrase, "Money can't buy happiness," never paid for a divorce.

My buddy broke his leg, so I went to visit him at his house. I came to find out that he has two gorgeous twin sisters. I went up to his room and asked him how he was doing. He said, "I'm okay but could you do me a huge favor and get my socks from downstairs? My feet are freezing!" So, I went downstairs and found his twin sisters sitting on the couch, right next to his socks. I told them, "Your brother sent me down here to have sex with both of you." They responded, "No way! Prove it!" I shouted upstairs, "Hey buddy! Both of them?" He shouted back, "Of course, both of them!" What's the point in fucking just one?!"

What is Superman's greatest weakness? A bucking horse!

Rice, when you want to eat two thousand of the same thing!

What's the difference between a blonde and a mosquito? A mosquito stops sucking when you slap it!

What do you call ten Mexicans in a barn? Antique farm equipment!

What do a woman and a bucket of KFC have in common? Once you're done with the breasts and the thighs, all that you're left with is greasy box to put your bone in!

Did you hear the joke about Jim Jones and Jonestown? Never mind, the punch line is too long!"

If I wanted to hear from an asshole, I'd fart!

What's one of the most embarrassing things in the world? Locking your keys in the car in front of the abortion clinic and having to go inside to ask for a coat hanger!

Did you ever blow bubbles as a kid? I saw him the other day, he said to say hi!

I got fired from my job today at the funeral home because I kept asking the customers, "Would prefer smoking, or non-smoking?" Apparently, the correct terms are 'cremation' and 'burial'!

What's the difference between your girlfriend and your wife? About 45 pounds!

My cat's dead. Can I play with your pussy instead?

My mother never saw the irony in it, every time that she called me a "Son of a bitch!"

Did you hear about the man who died of a Viagra overdose? They couldn't close his casket!

A seriously ill man is lying in a hospital bed on a ventilator. The man's family and the hospital chaplain gather around to comfort him. The man gestures for a pen and paper, writes a brief note, hands it to the chaplain, and then dies. The chaplain reads out the man's dying words to the people there, "HELP-YOU'RE STANDING ON MY BREATHING TUBE YOU DICK!"

Unexpected sex is a great way to be woken up, unless you're in prison!

What's the difference between three dicks and a joke? Your mom can't take a joke!

Why do old people smile all the time? Because they can't hear a fucking word that you're saying!

My friend asked me if I had to have sex with my mom to save my father's life what would I do? Apparently, 'Reverse Cowgirl' was an inappropriate answer!

People who are afraid of pedophiles need to grow up!

How do you use the word 'Cherokee' as a Mexican? "I lost my house key and now I have to 'Cherokee' with my sister!"

What's the most confusing day in Puerto Rico? Father's Day!

Did you hear about the gay security guard who got fired from his job at the sperm bank? He got caught drinking on the job.

When I was a kid, my mother told me that I could be anyone that I want to be. It turns out that identity theft is a CRIME!

What's the difference between black prisoners doing hard labour and snow tires? Snow tires don't sing when you put chains on them!

An old is lady taking a shower and starts to think about old times, and she gets a little bit frisky. She then gets out of the shower and puts her bath robe on. She walks into the bedroom, where her husband is sitting on the corner of the bed. She whips open her bathrobe in front of him and says seductively, "Super-pussy!" He replies, "I'll have the soup."

I'm as bored as a slut on her period!

You're not fat, you're just really easy to see!

What do you call a Mennonite with his arm up a horse's ass? A mechanic.

How do you fit an elephant into your car? Starve it to death and then chop it up into tiny little pieces.

Did you hear about the gay guy who couldn't tell K-Y Jelly from window putty? He was constipated for days, and all the windows fell out of his house.

A man leans towards a very attractive woman at the bar and asks, "Haven't I met you somewhere before?" The woman replies in a very loud voice, "Yes, you have. I'm the receptionist at the STD clinic!"

I stuck my head out of my car window and then I got arrested for 'Mooning'.

Crazy ex-girlfriends are like chocolate. They both will kill your dog!

A man says to his buddy, "My wife is really kinky, she likes to have sex in her ear." The friend asks, "Why is that?" The man replies, "Every time that I try to put it in her mouth, she turns her head!"

Why did the ghost go to rehab? He was addicted to boos!

My wife and I laugh about how competitive we are. But...I laugh more!

What do you say when your friend's breath smells like shit? "I'm bored, let's go brush our teeth!"

My friend gave me his "Epi-pen' as he was dying. It seemed very important to him that I have it!

I was kidnapped by mimes once. They did unspeakable things to me!

What do the movies, "The Titanic" and "The Sixth Sense" have in common? Icy dead people!

What happened to the snowman when he had a tantrum? He had a MELTDOWN!

How do you make the number '7' even? You take away the 's'.

I have a clean conscious. It's never been used!

What did the full glass say to the empty glass? "You look drunk!"

A guy walks into a public restroom and sees this man with no arms standing next to the urinal. The man asks, "Hey buddy, can you help me out and unzip my zipper?" The guy says, "OK." Then the man asks, "Can you pull it out for me?" The guy says, "OK." The guy pulls out the man's dick and it has mold and scabs all over it and it smells awful. The man takes a piss with the guy pointing it at the urinal. Then the guy puts the man's dick back into his pants. The guy asks, "What the hell is wrong with your dick?" Then the man pulls out his arms from his shirt and says, "I have no fucking idea, but there's no way that I'm touching it!"

I went to a zoo yesterday. They only had one animal. It was a dog. It was a Shih Tzu.

What do you call a hooker that likes anal sex? 'A crack whore!'

I said to my best friend, "I know this guy that sounds like an owl". He replied, "Who?"

Have you ever smelled moth balls before? How did you get their tiny little legs apart?

After 20 years of marriage, I still get blow jobs! But if my wife finds out, she'll fucking kill me!

Whenever I have a one-night stand, I use protection. A fake name and a fake phone number!

Vending machines are so homophobic! I'm sorry that my dollar is not straight enough for you!

Why is it called, 'taking a dump' when you're actually leaving one?

What do you call a magician who's lost his 'magic'? Ian.

I tripped over a bra. It was a goddamned booby trap!

My girlfriend's dad asked me, "What do you do?" Apparently, "Your daughter" wasn't the correct answer.

What's long, hard, and full of seamen? A submarine, you pervert!

I went up to a girl in the bar last night and said, "You're a big lass, aren't you?" She replied, "Tell me something that I don't know." I said, "Salad tastes good!"

Are you a trampoline? Because I want to bounce on you!

A man asks his butler, "Larry, call me a prostitute." Larry replies, "Sir, you're an ugly prostitute!"

I'm about three years into my relationship and now I've started to have some erection difficulties. My girlfriend and I differ on what the cause of the problem is. She bought me some Viagra and I bought her a treadmill!

What do you call a deer with no eyes? No eye deer! (Shrug shoulders with palms pointed up.)

Did you fall from heaven? Because it looks like you landed on your face!

A horse walks into a bar and the bartender asks, "Why the long face?" The horse, incapable of reasoning and understanding the human language, shits on the floor and then walks out of the bar.

What do hamsters and cigarettes have in common? They're completely harmless unless you put one in your mouth and light it on fire!

What did the banana say to the vibrator? "Why are you shaking? She's going to eat me!"

I had a big mix up at the department store today. Apparently when the clerk said, "Strip down, facing me", she was referring to my credit card.

A Scotsman stumbles out of a bar blind drunk wearing his kilt. Then he wanders to the nearest alleyway and sits down and falls asleep. A few minutes later, two college girls leave the bar and see the Scotsman sleeping there. The one girl asks the other, "I wonder if it's true that Scotsmen don't wear underwear?" The other girl says, "Let's see." She lifts up the Scotsman's kilt, and sure enough, he's not wearing any underwear. The girl then unties a blue ribbon from her hair and ties it around the Scotsman's penis. Then the girls run off while giggling. The next morning, the Scotsman wakes up and he has to take a piss like a racehorse. He lifts up his kilt to pee and sees the blue ribbon tied around his pecker. He says, "I don't know what we did last night, Laddy, but it looks like we won first prize!"

Why is a dog like a tree? Because they both lose their bark when they are dead!

The coroner was a very dedicated worker. He even went to work after he died!

A guy goes to a psychiatrist. He says, "Doc, I keep having this crazy recurring dream! First, I'm a Teepee, and then I'm a Wigwam. Then I'm a Teepee, and then I'm a Wigwam. I dream it over and over and over. What's wrong with me?" The psychiatrist replies, "It's simple, you're two tents!"

Your Mama is so damned fat that when I pictured her in my head, she broke my neck!

What do you call a Hippie's wife when at a formal event? 'Mississippi'.

My friend at work just told me about an article that he had read. Apparently, there's a spot on a woman's body that if you hit it just right, you can make her legs turn to Jelly. It's called, 'the chin!'

Did you hear about the man with five penises? His pants fit like a glove!

What's the difference between a watermelon and a dead hooker? The watermelon didn't scream when I sliced it up!

Have you heard of the book, "Parachuting from a plane?" Written by Hugo Furst.

How do you know if you're a true stoner? You wash your bong more than you wash your dishes!

I always go 'The extra mile.' The restraining order says that I have to!

How many potheads does it take to screw in a lightbulb? "Fuck it, just use a lighter!"

The thing about 'Your mom jokes" is that they're overly used... Just like your mom!

What's the best form of birth control for old people? Nudity!

So, I asked my North Korean friend how his life was going. He said to me, "I can't complain!"

What did the redneck you do when he saw his mother-in-law wandering around in the backyard with half a face? He stopped laughing and reloaded!

What's the difference between a blonde spinning herself around in a swivel chair and the Panama Canal? The Panama Canal is a busy ditch.

Why don't little pigmy kids play in the sandbox? The cats bury them.

What do you call a bunch of Puerto-Ricans running down a hill?   A prison break!

This summer I learned that there's a difference between peeing in the pool and peeing INTO the pool!

When you're at the playground with your fat friend, there are no seesaws, there are only catapults!

I love admiring statues! They show me what famous people would look like after I smear pigeon shit all over their faces.

'Hot Potato' is a very difficult game to play with Ethiopians.

What's the difference between a blonde and a bowling ball? You can only fit three fingers into a bowling ball!

What do gay guys call hemorrhoids? Speed bumps!

Your mom is so stupid that she put cat food down the front of her pants to feed her pussy!

What's the difference between a Harley and a Hoover? The position of the dirt bag!

A family walks into a hotel and the dad rushes up to the desk and leans over and asks the clerk, "Is the porn disabled?" The clerk looks at him and says, "No! It's regular porn, you sick bastard!"

What's the difference between your wife and your job? After 10 years, you job still sucks!

Your mom has a weight problem. She can't wait to eat!

Do you know that pigeons die after they have sex? The last pigeon that I fucked died!

Why are children like drums? Because the harder that you hit them, the louder that they get.

Is that a mirror in your pocket? Because I can see myself in your pants!

A Jew, an Italian and a Polish person are waiting to be executed by the electric chair. The Jew sits in the chair first. The warden asks him, "Do you have any last words?" The Jew says nothing. The warden then flips the switch. Nothing happens. The warden says, "You lucky son of a bitch, there's a one in a million chance that this electric chair doesn't work, you're free to go." The exact same thing happens with the Italian, and he's freed. When the Polish guy is sitting in the chair, the warden asks him, "Do you have any last words?" The Polish guy says, "Yes! Isn't this chair supposed to be plugged in?"

What comes after death? A necrophiliac!

How did the redneck find his sister in the field? Satisfying!

How do you get a one-armed blonde hanging from a tree branch down? Wave hello.

Why do Italian tanks have forward gear? In case they get attacked from the rear.

Why don't cannibals eat clowns? Because they taste funny.

What's the hardest thing about rollerblading? Telling your parents that you're gay!

What's 30 feet long and smells like urine? Line dancing at the nursing home!

What do cow patties and cowgirls have in common? The older that they get, the easier they are to pick up!

How did the blonde break her leg while she was raking leaves? She fell out of the tree!

Two mice are chewing on a roll of movie film at the library. The one mouse says to the other, "I think that the book was better!"

Knock, knock. Who's there? The mailman. The mailman who? You are so fucking dumb!

Why did the girl cross the road? Because I was following her!

A wife comes home late one night and opens the door to her bedroom. She lifts up the sheets at the bottom of the bed and she sees 4 legs instead of her husband two legs. She grabs a baseball bat and starts beating the bed with it in a fury. Once she's done, she goes to the kitchen and sees her husband sitting at the table. He says, "Hi darling, your parents came over for a surprise visit and I let them sleep in our bedroom!"

Accordion to a recent survey, replacing words with the names of musical instruments often goes undetected.

When you say the word 'poop', your mouth makes the same motion as your asshole. The same is true when you say the words, "Explosive diarrhea!"

There is no 'I' in denial!

How do you stop a clown from smiling? Shoot him in the face!

My retarded brother was as quick as a tree, and as sharp as a bowling ball. R.I.P.

Your wife is so fat that you have to roll over her twice to get to the other side of the bed!

A guy asks his buddy, "What starts with 'F' and ends with 'UCK?'" His buddy says, "What?" The guy replies, "Your answer is incorrect. 'What' begins with a 'W' and ends with 'HAT'."

A police officer pulls over a car that was diving around erratically. He approaches the car, and the driver rolls down his window and there is a distinct smell of marijuana wafting out of the window. The policeman asks the driver, "How high are you?" The stoner says, "No officer, it's hi, how are you?"

What do you call 10 midgets having a party? 'A little get together!"

Why do Jewish men like to watch porno movies in reverse? Because they like it when the hooker gives the money back!

Why do Asian women have small boobs? Because only A's are acceptable!

If the whole world smoked a joint at the same time, there would be world peace for at least two hours, followed by a global food shortage!

What's black and fuzzy and hangs from the ceiling? A blonde electrician!

You don't need a parachute to go skydiving once. But do you need a parachute if you want to go skydiving twice!

I had my mood ring stolen. As of now, I don't know how I feel about that.

Let's play carpenter! First, we'll get hammered, and then I'll nail you!

There was a cruise ship that sank off the coast of a deserted island. There were only three survivors, two guys and a girl. They all lived there for a couple of years doing what was natural for men and women. After several years of casual sex with the guys the girl became depressed and she felt guilty about what she had been doing, to the extreme that she killed herself. It was hard on the guys, but after a while, nature once again took its inevitable course, and the guys were having sex again. Well, after another couple of years the guys began to feel horrible about what they were doing. So, they decided to bury her!

The birth control pill...The second-best thing that a woman can put in her mouth to avoid getting pregnant!

My wife's sister knocked me out yesterday. I was furious! Who the hell puts chloroform on their dirty panties?"

I was so embarrassed when I got an erection during my prostate exam. But my doctor was very nice about it. He even put both of his hands on my shoulders to comfort me during the exam!

A naked wife looks into a mirror and says to her husband, "I look fat and ugly. Could you please pay me a compliment?" The husband answers, "Your eyesight is very excellent!"

What's the difference between roast beef and pea soup? Anyone can roast beef!

How do you have sensual sex with a camel? One hump at a time.

Don't you hate it when you're reading a sentence and it doesn't end the way that you 'TESTICLES!'

What do you call a bunch of retarded kids in a pool? Vegetable soup!

What do you call a rabbit with a crooked dick? 'Fucks Funny!'

Why are the majority of Italians in New York named Tony? Because when they got onto the boat to immigrate to America the officials stamped, 'TO NY' on their foreheads!

Why are cowgirls bowlegged? Because cowboys like to eat with their hats on!

What do you call a gay 'drive by shooting?" A fruit rollup!

What has a lot of little white balls and fucks old ladies? A bingo machine!

My girlfriend asked me why I was blow drying my crotch. Apparently, "I'm heating up your dinner" wasn't an intelligent answer.

Two hunters are out in the woods when one of them falls out of his tree stand. His friend goes to check on him and his buddy's eyes are glazed and he's unresponsive. The friend calls '911' and says, "I think that my friend is dead, what do I do?" The operator says, "Calm down, I can help. First, let's make sure that he's dead." There is a short silence, and then a gunshot rings out. The friend then asks the '911' operator, "Okay, now what?"

Why are hurricanes normally named after women? Because initially they come in wild and wet but then they eventually take your home and car!

What's worse than waking up after passing out at a redneck party and finding a penis drawn on your face? Finding out that your sister traced your brothers dick there with a permanent marker.

A boyfriend is showing off his new sportscar to his girlfriend. He asks her, "If I go 200 mph in this car will you get naked?" She responds, "Absolutely!" So, he gets the car up to 200 mph and she then strips down completely naked. The boyfriend is unable to keep his eyes on the road and drives over the shoulder and flips the car over. She gets flown out of the car and he gets stuck under the steering wheel. He yells, "Go and get help!" She says, I can't, I'm naked!" He says, take my shoe to cover yourself then." Holding the shoe over her privates she makes her way to a service station and says to the attendant, "Please help me! My boyfriend's stuck!" The attendant replies, "I'm sorry ma'am, but I can't help you. He's in there way too deep!"

Dr. Watson walks into a room and sees Sherlock Holmes having sex with a young girl. He asks, "Sherlock, is that a high school girl?" Holmes replies, "Elementary, my dear Watson!"

What do a 9-volt battery and a woman's asshole have in common? You know it's wrong, but sooner or later you're going to stick your tongue on it!

Three little old ladies are sitting on a park bench, when a man wearing a trench coat walks up and flashes them. The first old lady had a stroke. Then the second old lady had a stroke also. But the third old lady couldn't reach that far!

What do your mom and a used car have in common? They both have a lot of mileage, but I absolutely love taking them both for a ride!

What did the Jewish child molester say to the little boy at the truck stop? "Hey, little boy, want to buy some candy?"

Today at work my co-workers accused me of smearing feces everywhere! They're always blaming me for shit!

As I slipped my finger into her hole, I could immediately feel it getting wetter and wetter! I took my finger out and she immediately started going down on me! I said to myself, "I really fucking need to buy a new boat!"

Why do lazy men buy blow-up dolls from Iraq? Because they blow themselves up!

Little Johnny asks his dad, "What's the difference between hypothetical and reality?" Little Johnny's dad says to him, "Okay Johnny. I'll answer this question with a little demonstration. Little Johnny, go and ask your mom if she'd fuck the mailman for one million dollars." Little Johnny goes and asks his mom the question and she answers, "In an instant!" Little Johnny runs to his dad and says, "She said that she'd fuck him". The dad then says, "Okay Johnny, go and ask your sister the same question." Little Johnny asks his sister if she'd fuck the mailman for one-million dollars and she says, "In a heartbeat!" Little Johnny relays this answer to his dad. His dad then says, "Go and ask your brother the same question." Little Jonny comes back and says, "He said that he and the mailman would make a great couple and that they could travel with the money." Little Johnny's dad says, "Well son, hypothetically we're sitting on three million dollars here, but in reality, we're living with two whores and a faggot!"

What's a rednecks' definition of relative humidity? The sweat running down his balls while he's fucking his sister.

How do you turn a fox into an elephant? Marry her.

If Jack helped you off of the horse, would you help "Jack off the horse?"

The older that I get the more that I want to have sex with two women at the same time. After I'm done fucking them, they can spend time talking to each other while I grab a much-needed nap.

I really loved church when I was a kid. There was one thing that I did hate about it though, it was all of the standing up, sitting down and kneeling. I wish that the priest would just pick a position and fuck me already!

The only problem with phone sex is fitting the phone up your ass!

What's warm, wet, and pink? A fat redneck girl in a hot tub.

Please tell your tits to stop looking at my eyes!

I recently watched a freaky video of a girl having sex with fruit. To me, that's 'fucking bananas!'

My girlfriend told me that the best sex is, 'make-up sex.' So, I shoved her lipstick up my ass!

Women are catching up to men in equality but there are four areas that they'll never surpass guys at. Rape, murder, suicide, and being funny!

What's the first step in most Mexican recipes? Step one: Steal a chicken!

A man moves into a new house and his next-door neighbour comes over to greet him. He says, "Why don't I throw you a welcoming party tonight? My parties are awesome, there's always a lot of booze, drugs, and crazy sex!" The man says, "Wow! That would be great! What should I wear?" His neighbour says, "Whatever you want, it'll be just you and me!"

I woke up my wife at three am this morning and told her that I was so stressed out that only a blowjob could help me. She replied, "Where the fuck are you going to find a dick to suck at this time in the morning!"

Women only call me ugly until they find out how much money that I make. After that, they call me ugly and poor!

Apparently, someone in London gets stabbed every fifty-two seconds. I feel sorry for that poor bastard. I'm even considering donating him blood!

I feel bad for the homeless guy. But I even feel worse for the homeless guy's dog. The dog must be thinking, "This is the longest walk that I've ever had!"

Two Polish men are on opposite sides of the river. One shouts to the other, "I need to get to the other side!" The other Pollack yells back, "You are on the other side, you idiot!"

What do Dale Earnhardt and Pink Floyd have in common? Their latest big hit was, "The Wall!"

What's soft and warm when you go to bed, but hard and stiff when you wake up? Vomit.

How could the redneck mom tell that her daughter was on her period? She could taste blood on her son's cock.

My swimming instructor asked me what my favorite stroke was. Apparently, 'The one that killed Margaret Thatcher' wasn't the proper answer!

There was a sign outside the grocery store that said that you only need to wear masks and gloves while shopping during the Covid-19 pandemic. They lied! Apparently, you're supposed to wear clothes too!

An old couple are sleeping in bed at 4 AM in the morning when the old man rips out a loud fart for four seconds, and it wakes them both up. The old lady looks at her husband and asks, "What the hell was that?" He says, "Touchdown!" She asks, "What?" He says, "Seven points, touchdown!" She says, "Okay," and farts back. She says, "Seven points, tie game!" The husband is not going to lose to his wife in this contest, so he farts again and says, "Touchdown, fourteen to seven!" She farts back again and says, "Tie game!" Annoyed, the old man squeezes his butt cheeks hard, and then this horrible bubbling sound comes out and he shits the bed. The wife asks him, "What the hell was that?" He says, "Halftime, switch sides!"

I got fired from my zookeeper job because of a recent surge of dead animals. Apparently, the sign 'Don't feed the animals' was only meant for the visitors.

Stephen Hawking came back from a date night with broken glasses, a broken wrist, a twisted ankle, and grazed knees. Apparently, his date stood him up.

I broke up with my cross-eyed girlfriend for a good reason. Apparently, she was seeing someone else on the side!

I bought a new deodorant stick today. The instructions on it said, "Remove the cap and push up bottom." I did exactly as the instructions said, and now I can barely walk. But whenever I fart, the room smells lovely!"

Confucius say: Jerking off with peanut butter will make you come in a 'Jiffy'!

Somebody stole my antidepressants. Whoever did it, I hope that you're happy!

What do the Starship Enterprise and toilet paper have in common? They both go around Uranus and wipe out Klingons!

What's black and doesn't work? Decaffeinated coffee, you racist!

Why don't cannibals eat divorced women? Because they taste bitter!

How do Mexicans cut their pizza? With 'Little Caesars'!

A guy gets shipwrecked on a celebrity cruise and wakes up on a deserted island with Nicole Kidman. After a few weeks of being alone together on the island, they begin having passionate sex. This goes on for a while, but then the guy starts to become very depressed. Nicole asks him, "Why are you so upset?" The guy says, "I love being on a tropical island with as beautiful and lovely a woman as you, but I miss my friends. I miss my time at the bar with them." Nicole says, "Well, I'm an actress. Maybe if I get dressed in some of those men's clothes that got washed on the beach, I can pretend that I'm one of your guy friends and we can pretend that we're talking at the bar." This suggestion sounded strange to the guy, but he was open to it. Nicole then gets dressed into the men's clothes and asks the guy, "How are things?" The guy says, "Hey Nick, you'll never guess who I've been fucking!"

Your teeth are the whitest that I've ever come across.

What do you call a cow with no legs? Ground beef!

My wife isn't speaking to me, because I apparently ruined her birthday. I'm not sure how I did it, I didn't even know that it was her birthday!

A guy decides to ask his mailman, "What's the difference between an elephant's butthole and a mailbox?" The mailman answers, "I don't know?" The guy says in disgust, "I'm never getting you to mail a letter!'"

A customer is in a store and asks the clerk, "What aisle is the Polish sausage in?" The clerk asks the customer, "Are you Polish?" The customer, visibly offended, responds, "Yes. I am Polish. But If I asked you for Italian sausage, would you ask me if I was Italian? If I asked for bratwurst, would you ask if I was German?" The clerk responds, "Probably not." So, the customer then asks, "Then why did you ask me if I was Polish?" The clerk replies, "BECAUSE YOU'RE IN THE HOME DEPOT!"

The other day I spotted an albino dalmatian. I was very satisfied. It was my good deed for the day.

How do you sink a Polish warship? Put it in water!

A husband tells his Jewish wife that he wants her to be more vocal when they have sex. He says to her, "I'd love to hear some more moaning while we're in the sac, it really turns me on!" His wife agrees to this. Later that night, the couple starts getting it on, and then the wife proceeds to say to her husband, "That lamp on the nightstand is filthy and needs dusting, the paint on the ceiling is starting to peel and the curtains are disgustingly gross!"

What do you call a Polish fisherman? A fishing Pole!

Tom finds an old, tarnished lamp. He gets excited and polishes it. A genie appears and grants Tom three wishes. The genie asks Tom, "What's your first wish?" Tom says, "I want to be rich!" The genie says, "Done! Now what is your second wish, Rich?"

Apparently, the bible says that the proper punishment for adultery is to be stoned. That's why I always smoke a joint after I fuck my secretary!

A horse walks into a bar and the bartender asks, "Why the long face?" The horse relies, "It's because my wife is dying of terminal cancer."

Why did grandpa climb up the telephone pole with a backpack full of bananas? Because grandpa had dementia!"

What did Terrell Owens get on his SAT's? Barbeque sauce.

My grandma always said, "Slow and steady wins the race." My grandma died in a house fire!

Roses are red, violets are blue, I have Alzheimer's disease… "Cheese on toast!"

Why did the little girl's ice cream cone melt? Because she was on fire!

Why don't gay guys drive their Subaru's faster than 68 MPH? Because if they get to 69, they blow a rod!

A Pollack, a Chinese man and a Mexican are all working together on a roof. They all sit down together to have lunchbreak. The Polack opens his lunchbox and takes out a ham and cheese sandwich. He says angrily to his workmates, "This is the same lunch that I get every day. If I get this same ham and cheese sandwich again tomorrow, I'm going to jump off this roof in protest!" The Chinese man then opens his lunchbox and sees that he has noodles, as always. He says, "If I get noodles again tomorrow, I'm going to jump off of this roof too!" The Mexican takes out rice and beans from his lunchbox for the umpteenth time and he also proclaims that he'll jump off the roof if he gets the same lunch tomorrow. The next day arrives, and at lunchtime the Chinese man gets noodles and decides to jump to his death. The Mexican gets rice and beans again, and he also decides to jump to his death. As predicted, The Polack gets a ham and cheese sandwich for lunch. He furiously runs full speed towards the edge of the roof and jumps off and flies at least one-hundred feet towards his death. There was a mass funeral for the three men. The three mourning wives were all gathered together and reflected on the sad situation. The crying Chinese wife says, "I miss my husband. If I had just made something besides noodles for lunch, my husband would still be alive!" The distraught Mexican wife says, "I should have made my husband tacos instead of rice and beans. How can the pool boy and I afford living expenses without him?" The Polish wife is laughing hysterically. The other two wives ask her how could she be laughing at such a time as this? The Polish wife responds, "Because my husband always made his own lunch!"

What do you call a Chinese Priest? 'Ho Li Fuk!'

How do you know if a Chinaman has robbed your house? Your homework is done, your computer is updated and two hours later, the poor bastard is still trying to back out of your driveway!

Boobs are like the sun. You can only stare at them for only a very short time, but if you wear sunglasses you can stare at them for as long as you want!

Two Polish pilots are landing a plane. The plane hits the runway, but they don't have enough room and the plane crashes into the terminal. One pilot says to the other, "Man. That was a short runway!" The other pilot responds, "Yeah, but it sure was really wide!"

A man goes for his prostate exam and the doctor asks him to take off his pants. The man then takes off his pants and asks the doctor, "Where should I put these pants?" The doctor replies, "Put them on that hook right over there, right beside my pants!"

If your uncle Jack was up on the roof, and he needed you to help him down, would you help your uncle Jack off?"

What do a pizza boy and gynecologist have in common? They can both smell it, but they can't eat it!

How many Mexicans does it take to change a lightbulb? Just Juan.

Can you use the word, 'wheelchair' as a Mexican? "There's only one piece of pizza left, but, 'wheelchair'!"

Can you use the word 'mushroom' as a Mexican? "You can come for a ride in my car, but there's not 'mushroom'!"

Can you use the word 'bishop' as a Mexican? "Can somebody please shut this 'bishop'?"

If there are three apples and Little Johnny takes away three of them, how many apples does Little Jonny have? None, because Little Johnny got hit by a train!

What's the difference between Hitler and Logan Paul? At least Hitler had respect for the Japanese!

Did you know that Michael Jackson didn't die of a heart attack? He died of food poisoning. He ate a nine-year-old wiener. He also ate twelve-year old nuts!

How many Puerto Ricans does it take to shingle a roof? Seven if you slice them thin enough!

Why doesn't Jesus play hockey? He's afraid of getting nailed to the boards!

The bird, the bee and the running child are all the same thing to the sliding glass door!

I wonder what the word for 'dots' looks like in braille?

How did the blonde die while drinking milk? The cow fell on her.

Your mom is so ugly that she's like the sun. If you look at her too long, you'll go blind!

How do you kill a retard? Hand him a knife and ask him, "Who's special?"

Knock, knock. Who's there? Little boy blue. Little boy blue who? Michael Jackson!

Knock, knock. Who's there? Shmel-mipe. Shmel-mipe who? Sorry, I'm not kinky like that!

Knock, knock. Who's there? Little old lady. Little old lady who? I didn't know that you could yodel!

What do you do if a blonde throws a grenade at you? Pull the pin and throw it back!

Apparently, restaurants have been using lower quality ingredients during the Covid-19 pandemic to save money. I eat at a restaurant every day, but I haven't been able to taste anything for weeks!

My wife asked me which one of her friends would I like to have a threesome with. Apparently, I was only supposed to pick one!

Why do blondes wear shoulder pads? "I don't know!" (While smashing your head on either shoulder multiple times!)

How do blondes commit suicide? They put spikes on their shoulder pads!

Why does the Easter Bunny hide his easter eggs? Because he doesn't want anyone to know that he's been fucking the chicken!

Why are there only two pallbearers at a redneck funeral? Because there are only two handles on a garbage can!

Apparently, drinking a pint of beer shortens your life by nine minutes. According to my calculations, I should have died sometime in 1829!

A Polack, a Jew and an Englishman were all taken prisoner by rebels in Europe. They were all sentenced to death by firing squad. The day of the execution came, and the Jew stood up against the firing wall. The Jew suddenly points and shouts out, "Tornado!" The firing squad turns to look, and the Jew runs away. Then it was the Englishman's turn. He yelled, "Flood!", and he escaped as well. Then it was the Polacks turn. He placed himself against the wall in front of the firing squad and yelled, "Fire!"

What do you call a chicken looking into a bowl of lettuce? "Chicken-sees-a-salad!"

Apparently, there's a new medicine out there that cures skepticism. Well, I'm not buying it!

Your mama is so fat that when she walked in front of the TV, I missed three episodes of 'Fat Albert'!

I ran for three miles today. Finally, I stopped and said, "Lady, you can have your purse back!"

What do you call a blonde with half of a brain? Gifted!

I thought that getting a vasectomy would prevent pregnancy. Apparently, it only changes the colour of your baby.

I just got kicked out of a gender reveal party. Apparently, I was supposed to wear pants!

You are the reason that the gene-pool needs a lifeguard!

Knowledge is knowing that a tomato is a fruit. Wisdom is not putting tomatoes in your fruit salad!

A teacher asks her students, "Kids, what does the chicken give you?" The children answer in unison, "MEAT!" "Very good!", says the teacher. "Now, what does the pig give you?" The class replies, "BACON!" The teacher then says, "Great! Now what does the fat cow give you?" The kids all shout out at the same time, "HOMEWORK!"

I love what you've done with your hair! How did you get it to come out of your nostrils like that?

A computer once beat me at chess, but it was no match for me at kickboxing!

Going to church doesn't make you Christian any more than standing in a garage makes you a car!

I don't suffer from insanity… I enjoy every minute of it!

At every party there are two kinds of people. Those who want to go home and those that don't. The trouble is, they are usually married to each other!

Always borrow money from a pessimist. They'll never expect for you to pay it back!

The problem isn't that obesity runs in your family. It's that NO ONE runs in your family!

Opinions are like assholes. Everyone has one!

Spell IHOP and say 'nis' at the end.

I don't have a beer gut. I have a protective covering for my rock-hard abs!

A guy calls into work and says, "Hey boss, what's the difference between work and your daughter?" The boss asks, "What?" The guy says, "I'm not coming into work this morning!"

A baby seal walks into a club…

What do David Hasselhoff and a snowman in July have in common? They're both 'puddles'.

Your lips look lonely. Let me introduce them to mine!

Why do Jewish women like to have sex with the lights off? Because they never want to see a man having a good time!

What's the best part about a blowjob? Ten minutes of peace and quiet!

The only drinking problem that I have is that I can't afford alcohol!

Did Jesus die a virgin? No, he got nailed many times before he died!

Is your ass jealous about the amount of shit that comes out of your mouth?

A family was driving behind a garbage truck when a dildo flies out of the back of the truck hits the car's windshield. To spare her son and her any embarrassment the mom says, "Don't worry son, that was just a bug." The son replies, "I'm surprised that that bug could get off the ground and fly with a cock that big!"

I met this beautiful girl the other night. She said that her pussy tasted, "Like a rainbow." It turns out that she meant "Trout", not "Skittles!"

I'm always Frank with my sexual partners. I don't want them to know my real name!

An Italian girl just gets done having rough sex in the back of a rental car? She gets out, waves her hands, and says, "It's-a hurts!"

What does it mean when your boyfriend is your bed gasping for his breath and screaming you name? You didn't hold the pillow down on his face long enough!

The saying, "See a penny and pick it up, and all day you'll have good luck!" does not apply in a prison shower!

How did the Newphy get killed while ice fishing? He got run over by the Zamboni!

My girlfriend told me to give her 12 inches and hurt h, so I fucked her twice and hit her in the face with a brick!

How does Justin Bieber remove a condom? He farts!

My E-Harmony application was rejected. Apparently, the answer to question 14, "What do you like most in a woman?", wasn't supposed to be, "My dick!"

A ventriloquist is telling blonde jokes in a bar when a young lady in his audience stands up and complains. "I've heard just about enough of your lousy blond jokes!" she shouts. "What makes you think that you can stereotype women this way? What does a person's hair colour have to do with their worth as a human being?" The ventriloquist is very embarrassed and starts to apologize. The blonde interrupts him and says, "Stay out of it, mister! I'm talking to that little bastard sitting on your knee!"

I just got my dick stuck in my zipper, and God, does it ever hurt! No more zip up boots for me!

I got my family banned from Family Feud today. The category was, "Describe your sex life with a SpongeBob SquarePants quote." "ARE YOU READY KIDS!" was apparently the wrong answer.

A guy calls 911. He says, "I need help!" The 911 operator asks, "What's the problem?" The guy responds, "Well, there are two girls over here fighting over me!" The operator asks, "So, what's the emergency?" The guy says, "The ugly girl is winning!"

A man asks his friend, "How did you manage to quit smoking, cold turkey?" His friend replies, "I decided to smoke only after I have sex!

What did the Maxi-pad say to the fart? You are the wind beneath my wings!

A Scotsman stumbles up the stairs in a drunken stupor with a sheep under his arm. He opens the door to his bedroom and sees his wife sitting up in their bed. He says, "This is the pig that I've been fucking!" His wife replies, "You idiot! That's not a pig, that's a sheep!" The Scotsman says, "Shut up woman! I was talking to the sheep!"

A clitoris has 8000 nerve endings. But it is not as sensitive as a lesbian on social media!

I told my boss that three companies were after me and that I needed a raise to be able to stay at my job. He said, "Okay" and gave me a raise. Then he asked me, "Which three companies are after you?" I said, The gas company, the electric company, and the cable company!"

I got kicked out of the hospital today. Apparently, the sign that said, "Stroke patients here" had a completely different meaning!

BREAKING NEWS: Look alive people! We have reports of an escaped necrophiliac in your area!

I was chasing a fat girl who was holding a dildo in the park the other day. I would have left her alone if she had just given me back my dildo!

My fat neighbour Keith has breasts bigger that my wife's. That's because everyone has breasts bigger than my wife's!"

I asked my Scottish friend, "How many sexual partners have you had?" He started counting, but then he fell asleep!"

How do you know when a woman says something stupid? It's when she opens her mouth!

A woman goes to her doctor and complains about abdominal pain, thinking that she might be pregnant. After a physical examination, and interpreting her tests, the doctor comes out to speak to her and says, "Well, I hope that you don't mind changing diapers." She replies, "Oh my God! Am I pregnant!?" The doctor replies, "No, you have colon cancer."

Hitler visits a concentration camp and asks a boy prisoner, "How old are you?" The boy says, "I'll be six soon!" Hitler relies, "No, you won't!"

A boyfriend asks his bitchy girlfriend, "Did you fall from heaven? Because so did Satan!"

My girlfriend asked me, "How do you like babies?" Apparently, "It depends on how they're cooked" was the wrong answer.

Auto correct on text got me arrested for proclaiming my love to my crush. Apparently, stating, "I wish that you were nine" is considered a criminal offense.

What does Beethoven do in his coffin? He decomposes!

They say that there's safety in numbers. Tell that to 6 million Jews!

I asked to switch seats on a plane because I was sitting next to a screaming baby. Apparently, that's not allowed if the baby is yours!

What's black and blue and red and lies in a ditch? You after you disrespect me!

Every time that you make a 'typo' the 'errorists' win!

Why did the chicken cross the road? To get to the asshole's house. Knock, knock. Who's there? The chicken!

A guy asks his buddy, "What's the difference between a kid and a hooker?" His friend replies, "I don't know?" To which the guy says, "YOU SICK FUCK!"

I wish that my grass was 'emo' because then it would cut itself!

A son asks his dad, "Dad, why is this red soup so sweet?" The dad replies, "Because your mother had diabetes!"

How do you know if a redneck girl is a virgin? She can still outrun her brothers!

Why did they invent glow in-in-the dark condoms? So gay guys can have light saber duels just like they do in Star Wars!

A kid asks his dad, "Dad, what is dark humour?" His dad points to a man across the street and asks his son, "Do you see that guy over there across the street?" The son replies, "No dad, you know that I'm blind!" The dad says, "Son, that's dark humour!"

How do you drown a blonde? Put a 'scratch and sniff' sticker on the bottom of the pool!

What did the sniper say to his wife? "Honey, I missed you!"

Did you hear about the Jewish guy who walked into a wall with a hard-on? He broke his nose!

How do you get a nun pregnant? Dress her up like an altar boy!

Did you hear about the two-car pileup in Mexico? 200 Mexicans died!

Why did Sally fall off of the swing? Because she didn't have any arms! Knock, knock. Who's there? NOT SALLY!

Why was Helen Keller such a bad driver? Because she's a woman!

Jesus Christ fed two-thousand people with five loaves of bread and two fish. But Adolf Hitler made six million Jews toast!

What did the boy with no hands get for Christmas? Gloves! Just kidding, he hasn't unwrapped his present yet!

What's a pedophile's favorite thing about Halloween? Free delivery!

What does a woman with two black eyes say? Nothing, if she's smart!

A blonde walks into a doctor's office and tells him that her body hurts anywhere that she touches it. The doctor says, "Show me." The blonde pushes on her elbow with her finger and screams in agony. Then she pushes her finger on her knee and screams in agony. She then pushes on her ankle with her finger with the same response. The doctor asks the blonde if she's Polish. She replies, "No." The doctor then says, "I think that your finger is broken!"

What do Michael Jackson and a PlayStation have in common? They're both plastic and little kids turn them on!

Why do white people go to Puerto-Rican garage sales? To get their stuff back!

What did the blonde get on her I.Q. test? Saliva!

A guy tells his buddy, "I remember the first time that I used alcohol as a substitute for a woman." His buddy asks, "What happened?" The guy says, "I got my cock stuck in the neck of the bottle and had to smash it!"

How do you get twenty Mexicans into a phonebooth? Tell them that they own it. How do you get them out? Throw in a bar of soap!

What do you call a man with no arms and no legs sitting in a pile of leaves? Russell.

Why do Jews have such big nostrils? Because air is free.

What's the difference between Michael Jackson and acne? Acne doesn't come on a five-year old's face!

Why did the pedophile cross the road? To get to the other preschool!

I got banned from the paintball arena today. Apparently, they look down on using a knife to save ammo!

What do you call a man with no arms and no legs hanging on the wall? Art.

Your mom is so stupid that she brought her own spoon to the Super Bowl!

What did Helen Keller say when she fell off of a cliff? (Mimic sign language with jazz hands!)

What's the difference between preschool and a pedophiles basement? Little kids leave preschool.

In sex ed class, my teacher asked me, "What was missing in your first sexual experience?" Apparently, "Consent" was the wrong answer. The cops are on their way!

What's the difference between a washing machine and a blonde? I can put a load in the washing machine without it following me around!

Your mom is so ugly, that when she tried to register for an 'Ugly contest', they told her, "Sorry, no professionals!"

I've always said that one man's trash is another man's treasure. Apparently, that's not a good way to tell your kid that he's adopted.

What do you call a Mexican who doesn't have a lawn mower? Unemployed.

Your momma is so stupid that she climbed over a glass wall just to see what was on the other side!

Why did the blonde have sex with the Mexican boy? Because her teacher told her that he'd give her extra credit to do an 'essay'.

A mother and a daughter are walking down the beach when the daughter asks, "Mom, do you think that I should use a douche?" The mother answers, "Why don't you ask the seagulls that have been following you this whole time!"

A man was turned down for a job after his job interview. They asked him about his most recent example of successful teamwork. He answered, "Gang rape!"

Two condoms walk into a bar. The one says to the other, "Want to get shit faced?!"

Studies show that if women have one glass of wine a day it increases the chances of having a 'stroke'. If she has more than one glass, she might 'suck it' too!

What do you say to two identical twins who are in love with each other? "GO FUCK YOURSELF!"

What do a gynecologist's hand and KFC have in common? They're both 'FINGER LICKIN' GOOD!"

What did the husband say to his wife when she decided to give him a hand job? "Honey, you shouldn't play with your food!"

If a stork brings people babies, what bird takes them away? "The swallow!"

Three things that you hated when you were a kid, but you love as an adult:

1. Taking naps.
2. Reading.
3. Spankings!

Do you feel like fucking a STUD? Because I have the STD and all that I need is "U".

What did the crazy hooker say to the peanut when he requested her services? "I may be crazy, but I'm not fucking nuts!"

Opinions are like orgasms. Mine is more important and I don't care if you have one!

Why did my sperm cross the road? Because it was in the chicken!

How do you know if your girlfriend is getting fat? It's when she starts stealing your wife's clothes!

Apparently, one in three households live next to a pedophile. Not me though, I live between two smoking hot seven-year-olds!

I got rugburn on my dick from a blow job last night. The guy wouldn't take off his J-Lo mask!

Hippies don't screw in light bulbs. They screw in dirty sleeping bags in the woods!

I went to a nightclub the other night. First, they played the "Twist." Then they played the "Electric Slide." Then they played, "Come on Eileen." Now I'm banned from the nightclub and Eileen isn't talking to me anymore!

Two deaf lesbians are walking down the sidewalk with their hands down each other's pants. Apparently, they were 'lip reading!'

A guy goes to show his buddies that he has glitter on his balls after a night at the strip club. There was no glitter on his dick, just his balls. His buddies said, "Pretty nuts!"

Statistics show that 90% of women don't like me wearing pink shirts. That's ironic. Because 90% of men wearing pink shirts don't like women!

I asked a German girl for her phone number today. She said, "999-999-9999". That's a weird phone number!

I called the rape advice hotline today. Apparently, It's only for victims.

What did the blonde say when she looked into a box of Cheerios? "Doughnut seeds!"

What's the difference between a woman with PMS and a terrorist? You can negotiate with a terrorist!

What did the letter 'O' say to the letter 'Q'? Zip up your fly, your dick is hanging out!

A man walks into a bar and notices a big jar full of twenty-dollar bills on the counter. He asks the bartender, "What's up with that jar of money?" The bartender says, "There's a contest at this bar. If you pass the three tests of the contest, you win the money." The man then asks, "What are the three tests?" The bartender says, "See that massive man at the end of the bar? You must knock him out with one punch. Then, there is a rottweiler in the back room with a gold tooth. You must remove the gold tooth. And then there is a ninety-year-old lady in the apartment upstairs. You need to fuck her and make her have an orgasm. If you pass all the three tests, you'll get the money." The man says that he'll think about it and proceeds to get plastered in the meantime. He then accepts the challenge. He walks up to the giant man at the end of the bar and floors him with one punch. Then he goes into the back room. He's in there for a while, and there are awful sounds of roaring and screaming heard through the door. The man then walks out of the door, his clothes ripped and with scratches and bite marks all over him. He then asks the bartender, "Okay, I've completed two tasks so far. Now where's that old bitch with the gold tooth?

How do you make 5 pounds of fat look good? Put a nipple on it!

Rearrange these letters to form words. 1. PNEIS. 2. BUTTSXE. Did you get "Spine" and "Subtext?" No? Neither did I.

When someone tells me that I look familiar to them, I say, "Yep, I do porn!"

There is a new trend in my office. Everyone is putting their name on their food. I saw it today while I was eating a sandwich named, "Kevin."

My annual performance review said that I was lazy and that I lack, "Passion and integrity." I guess that the management team hasn't seen me alone with a Big Mac!

The only thing worse than seeing something done wrong is seeing it done slowly!

Some people say that the glass is half empty or that's it half full. That's irrelevant to me, because I'm having another drink!

You're so fat that you could sell shade!

What's the best thing about a Gypsy girl on her period? When you finger her, you get your palm read for free!

What's the difference between a walrus and a lesbian? One smells like a fish and has a moustache and the other is a walrus!

Apparently, I snore so loudly that I scare everyone in the car that I'm driving!

I got into a water fight with my next-door neighbours. They were no match for me and my kettle full of boiling water!

What's the difference between an epileptic corn farmer and a hooker with explosive diarrhea? One shucks and has fits!

Why did Bill Gates' wife leave him? His dick was micro-soft.

Your face looks like an asshole with teeth!

I used to go out with a girl who punched me in the face every time that she had an orgasm. I was okay with it until I found out that she was faking her orgasms!

I was walking down the road the other day and I saw a man who was trying to rape a girl. So, being the good Samaritan that I am, I decided to help. It was some of the best sex that I've ever had!

What do lesbian and turtles have in common? They both choke on plastic!"

Why were there no gay Egyptians? Because they all worshiped pussies!

I just met a girl with twelve nipples. Sounds unbelievable, dozen tit?

A guy was having sex with a blowup doll. Then he bit her tit, she farted and then flew out of the window!

What's the difference between Santa and 6 million Jews? Santa goes DOWN the chimney!

Why does a bride smile so much while walking down the aisle? Because she knows that she's given her last blowjob!

I've put on so much weight during the Covid-19 lockdown... now my girlfriend can cum on MY TITS!

You're so ugly that when your dog humps your leg, he closes his eyes!

Apparently, the year '666' was cursed. Everyone that was born that year is dead!

When your girlfriend seductively tells you, "You can stick it anywhere that you want", apparently, "In her roommate" was not one of the options!

A patient wakes up in a hospital bed with his doctor standing over him. The patient says in a panic, "Doctor, I can't feel my legs!" The doctor says, "I know, I amputated your arms."

If a tree falls in the forest and no one hears it, then my illegal logging company is a success!

My doctor told me that I was going deaf. The news was really hard to hear!

I just got back from a job interview where I was asked if I could perform "under pressure". I said that I wasn't too sure about that but that I could perform a wicked "Bohemian Rhapsody!"

Why do Asian people have slanted eyes? Because atomic bombs are really bright!

My girlfriend yelled at me for treating her like a child. Then I gave her a sticker for standing up for herself.

Apparently, my family is racist. I introduced my new black girlfriend to them, and they all started screaming at me. Especially my wife!

What did the blonde say when she found out that she was pregnant? "I hope that it's not mine!"

Apparently, I'm a bad listener. My wife sent me to the supermarket to buy a loaf of bread. She said, "And if they have eggs, get a dozen!" I came home with 12 loaves of bread. I still don't understand why she's angry with me!

You're so hairy that when you went skydiving everyone thought that you were a MAGIC CARPET!

I have a lot of growing up to do. I realized that the other day while I was inside my fort!

What's do a Jew and a hard nipple have in common? They both disappear after a hot shower!

Why is there so little Puerto Rican literature? Because spray-paint wasn't invented until 1949!

The early bird might get the worm, but the second mouse gets the cheese!

I like to hold hands at the movies, which always seems to startle the strangers!

How do you kill 100 Mexicans? Blow up their car!

The worst time to have a heart attack is during a game of Charades!

Does my wife think that I'm a control freak? I haven't decided yet!

You're so cheap that you can't even pay attention!

In class at my school, the teacher asked one her students to prove the law of gravity, so the kid threw the teacher out of the window!

An Italian and a Polish guy are walking down the beach, wearing Speedo bathing suits. The Italian guy received a lot of attention from the women that passed by them, but the Polish guy didn't get any attention. At the end of the day, the Polish guy asks the Italian, "You have to tell me your secret! I'm not bad looking, I'm physically fit, but you're the only one that got the girls' attention?" The Italian says, "Okay, tomorrow before we walk on the beach, put a potato in your Speedo." The next day they walk down the beach again, but the women still don't pay any attention to the Polish guy. That night, the Polish guy asks the Italian, "I put a potato in my Speedo, and nothing happened? What is your SECRET?" The Italian guy says, "Try putting the potato in the FRONT of your Speedo!"

Why did the redneck cross the road? Because he couldn't get his dick out of the chicken!

I just got punched in the face for trying to kiss my friends' new baby on the forehead. Apparently, I have to wait until the baby's born first!

What do you call an Ethiopian on a hunger strike? An 'Ethiopian'!

How do you know if a redneck girl is on her period? She's only wearing one sock.

How many Irishmen does it take to screw in a lightbulb? Two, one to hold the lightbulb in place and the other to drink until the room spins!

What do you get when you cross an elephant with a poodle? A dead poodle with an 18-inch asshole!

What do you call a fat Chinese person? 'A Chunk!'

What's the best thing about having sex with a homeless girl? When you're done, you can drop them off anywhere!

What do you call a man with no arms and no legs lying on the ground outside your front door? Matt.

Three men are at the pearly gates in front of Saint Peter on Christmas Eve waiting to gain entry. Saint Peter says to them, "You must each show me a symbol of Christmas and then you can enter into Heaven." The first man pulls a lighter out of his pocket and lights it and says, "This is a Christmas candle." Saint Pater lets him in through the gates. The second guy holds out his keys in front of him and shakes them and says, "These are Christmas bells." Saint Peter lets him in. The third guy is sweating bullets, but then he thinks of a fantastic solution. He pulls out a pair of pink panties from his back pocket and holds them up and says, "These are Carol's!"

What did the Jamaican boy scream to him mom while he was having diarrhea? "Mommy, I'm MELTING!"

What do priests and Santa Claus have in common? They both leave little boys' homes with empty sacs!

How did the Grand Canyon come into existence? A caravan of Jews lost a nickel there.

How do you tell who the head nurse is? She's the one with the dirty knees!

What's the difference between a Jew and a pizza? A pizza doesn't scream when you put it in the oven!

What did Hitler get his niece for her birthday? An Easy Bake Oven!

Why don't Puerto Ricans have check books? Because it's impossible to sign you name that small with spray-paint!

Pull out the skin on both sides of your neck and ask, "What's this?" An Ethiopian with a corn flake stuck in his throat!

What's better than winning gold in the Paralympics? Walking!

I used to be indecisive, but now I'm not sure.

What do you get when you cross Raggedy Ann with the Pillsbury Dough Boy? A redhead with a yeast infection!

Why did God give women three more brain cells than cows? So, they don't shit on the floor while they're doing the dishes!

How do you keep an Indian out of your back yard? Move the trash cans to the front yard!

How does a redneck girl keep the flies off of her food? She opens her legs!

What's the difference between a Jew and a canoe? A canoe tips!

My father was such a heavy drinker that when he blew on his birthday cake, he lit the candles!

I have an inferiority complex, but it's not a good one.

How does every racist joke start? With a look over both shoulders.

I just got banned from a Christian dating website today. Apparently, "HUNG_LIKE_JESUS" isn't an appropriate username!

My wife is so mad at me! She complained about how bad her C-section scar looked. Apparently, "Don't worry honey, your tits will cover it up eventually", was the wrong answer!

My girlfriend broke up with me for being too immature. I took a deep breath and calmed down. Then I went to her house and rang the doorbell and ran away!

Apparently, men think about sex every seven seconds. I make sure that I eat my hotdogs within six seconds so that it doesn't get weird!

Why don't Pakistanis play hockey? Every time that they go into the corner, they open up a store!

A passenger airplane is flying towards the airport for its final decent. The pilot turns on the intercom and says, "We're on our final descent and I want thank you all for flying with us. Enjoy you stay in New York." The pilot then neglects to turn off the intercom and says to his co-pilot, "When we land, I'm going to take a big shit and then fuck the hell out of Lucy, the new stewardess!" Everyone on the plane hears this. Lucy starts running towards the cockpit, trips and falls. An elderly woman next to her says, "No need to run honey. He's got to take a shit first!"

What do you call a man with no arms and no legs floating in a lake? Bob.

If you have ten apples in one hand and fourteen oranges in the other hand, what do you have? Really big hands!

A man walks into a lawyer's office and asks, "How much do you charge?" The lawyer says, "$5000 dollars for 3 questions." "Wow, that's pretty expensive?", says the man. "Yes", says the lawyer. Now, what's your third question?"

I can't take my dog to the park because the ducks keep biting him. I guess that's what I get for buying a pure bread dog!

I told my friend not to get too excited about turning 32 since her party would be short. She asked, "Why would it be short?" I said, "Because it's your 30-second birthday!"

My girlfriend asked me, "How do you view lesbians? Apparently, "In HD" was the wrong answer!

I believe that a duck's opinion of me depends on whether or not I have bread.

I bought a new thesaurus the other day. Not only is it terrible, it's also terrible!

What is the difference between Tom Cruise and a tuxedo? One comes out of the closet for gay adventures, and the other is a tuxedo.

Did you hear that Oprah Winfrey got caught at the airport for smuggling drugs? They lift up her dress and found four-hundred pounds of crack!

A kid says to his fat friend, "Hey fatty, why are you so fat?" The fat kid replies, "Because every time that I fuck the bejesus out of your mother, she bakes me a cake!"

You're so ugly that when your mom dropped you off at school, she got a ticket for littering!

I lost my job at the suicide hotline. Apparently, reverse psychology is not appropriate in that line of work!

I like to take a toothpick and throw it into the woods and yell, "You're home now!"

You're so ugly that I have to quit drinking, just so that I don't see two of you!

At a job interview they asked me, "Where do you see yourself in five years?" I told them, "I'll still be using a mirror five years from now!"

I tried to form a professional hide and seek team, but it was a failure. It turns out that good players are really hard to find!

Why should you never brush your teeth with your left hand? Because a toothbrush works much better!

My dad died because he couldn't remember his blood type. He kept saying, "be positive!" We will miss him dearly!

I tried to explain to my 4-year-old son that it's perfectly normal to accidentally poop in your pants. He's still making fun of me!

I wasn't very close to my father when he died, which is lucky because he died after stepping on a land mine!

A guy dressed up as a chicken for Halloween. He finds a girl dressed as an egg. Apparently, the answer is, "The chicken."

A pirate walks into a bar with a steering wheel shoved down the front of his pants. One of the bar's patrons is brave enough to ask, "Hey buddy, what's with the steering wheel down the front of your pants?" The pirate says, "Arrrgh, it's driving me nuts!"

What would Patrick Swayze be doing at this very moment if he were alive today? He'd be scratching at the lid of his coffin!

Why do they put shit on the wall at Pakistani weddings? To keep the flies off the bride!

Why don't birds wear underwear? Because they have their peckers on their face.

What do you call a dog with no hind legs and steel balls? Sparky!

Where did Christa McCullough, the schoolteacher who went on the Space Shuttle Challenger, take her vacation? All over Florida!

What was Christa McCullough's eye colour? Blue, one blew this way, and one blew that way!

What kind of shampoo did Christa McCullough use? Head and Shoulders. They found the evidence on the beach!

Why are Santa's balls so big? Because he only comes once a year, usually down the chimney!

What do you call thirty-six North American Indian women around a fire? A full set of teeth!

What's the difference between a walrus and an Eskimo woman? A walrus has more teeth!

The world is way to politically correct these days. You can't even say 'black paint' anymore. Now you have to say, "Jamal, would you please paint my fence?"

Why did Elliot Spitzer cheat on his wife? Because she was a 'Spitzer', not a 'Swallower'.

A man walks into a pharmacy and asks the pharmacist for birth control for his wife and his 11-year-old daughter. The pharmacist is shocked, and she asks him, "Is your daughter sexually active?" The man replies, "No, she kind of just lies there".

What's the difference between one-thousand dead babies and a Corvette? I don't have a Corvette in my garage.

Someone glued all of my playing cards together. I don't know how to deal with it!

What do you call a lesbian dinosaur? A lickalotypus!

What do you call a gay dinosaur? Megasoreass!

I don't trust those trees. They seem kind of shady! I'm going to call the tree removal service.

How do you catch an elephant? First, dig a hole that's bigger than the elephant. Then fill the hole full of ashes. Then, put peas all around the edge of the hole. So...when the elephant goes to take a pea, kick him in the ash-hole!

How do you know if your wife is dead? The sex is the same, but the dishes start to pile up!

Did you hear that Ellen DeGeneres almost drowned? They found her face down in Ricki Lake!

What's the definition of 'impossible'? Trying to nail diarrhea to the wall!

My girlfriend called me last night and told me that she had just been diagnosed with AIDS. The secret is... to act surprised.

A woman went into a store to buy her husband a pet for his birthday. After taking a look around the store, she discovered that all the pets were very expensive. She told the clerk that she wanted to buy a pet for her husband, but that she didn't want to spend a fortune. The clerk said, "Well, I have a very large bullfrog that's been trained to give blowjobs." The woman thought that it would be a great gag gift, and if the bullfrog actually gave blowjobs, she'd be off the hook for giving her husband blowjobs again. She bought the frog. She gave the bullfrog to her husband, but he was very skeptical and laughed it off. The couple then went to bed for the night. In the middle of the night the wife was awakened by the noise of pots and pans flying everywhere in the kitchen, making crashing sounds. She ran downstairs to the kitchen to find her husband and the bullfrog reading cookbooks. She asked them, "What the hell are you two doing this late at night?" The husband replied, "If I can teach this frog to cook, your fucking ass is out of this house!"

What were Jesus's last three words? "OW... OWW... OWWWWW!!!"

What do you call Tarzan in a tree with a briefcase? Branch manager.

Why do men have a hole at the end of their penis? So, that they can stay open minded!

What sexual position produces the ugliest children? Ask your mom!

How do you make your wife scream while having sex? Call her on the phone and tell her!

What's the difference between a golf ball and a g-spot? A guy will actually look for a golf ball!

How do you embarrass an archeologist? Give him a used tampon and ask him which period that it came from.

What did the pirate say when they asked him where his buccaneers were? He said, "They're under me BUCKING HAT!"

Why does Dr. Pepper come in a bottle? Because his wife died.

Which Smurf recycles? Smurfette, because she has a blue box!

What's the difference between an oral thermometer and a rectal thermometer? The taste!

What kind of bees make milk? Boobies!

How did the blonde chip her tooth? On the vibrator!

Two buddies are walking in the desert when one of them gets bit by a rattlesnake on this ass. He falls to the ground and asks for his buddy to go and get help. So, his buddy walks about two miles to a payphone and calls a doctor. He says to the doctor, "My buddy just got bit on the ass by a rattlesnake, what do I do?" The doctor tells him that he's going to need to suck the poison out of his friend's ass. The guy walks the two miles back to his buddy. His buddy asks, "What did the doctor say?" His friend replies, "The doctor said that you're going to die!"

What did Mr. and Mrs. Wong name their retarded baby? Sum Ting.

What's the definition of pain? Jumping off the CN Tower and landing on a bike with no seat!

When did Pinocchio realize that he was made of wood?   When his hand caught on fire!

What's green and smells like pork? Kermit the frog's finger.

Why don't bunnies make any sound while they're having sex? Because they have cotton balls!

A patient is in the examination room of a very attractive female doctor. She tells the patient, "I have bad news for you, you'll have to stop masturbating." The patient asks, "Why?" The doctor replies, "Because I'm trying to examine you!"

I was about to roll a joint with this cute Mexican girl. But then, when I asked her if she had any papers, she ran away!

How did the Newphy get killed while ice fishing? He got run over by the Zamboni!

What did the elephant say to the naked man standing in front of him? "How the fuck do you breathe through that thing!"

What did one lesbian frog say to the other lesbian frog? "We really do taste like chicken!"

What do Christmas trees and priests have in common? Their balls are for decoration only!

How did they invent streaking? They tried to give a Puerto Rican a bath!

What's the definition of agony? A one-armed man hanging from a cliff with itchy balls!

How do you babysit a Jamaican kid? Lick his lips and stick him to the wall! How do you get the Jamaican kid off of the wall? Slide him to a corner.

Who's the most popular guy in the nudist colony? The guy who can carry a dozen doughnuts and a cup of coffee in each hand, all at the same time!

What did the bird say when his cage broke? "Cheap, cheap, cheap!"

What's the difference between a lawyer and a carp? One is a scum sucking bottom feeder and the other is a fish!

How do you know if your house has been robbed by Pollacks? Your dog is pregnant, and your garbage is gone!

A Mexican and a Puerto-Rican are sitting in a car. Who's driving? The cops!

Why does Ellen DeGeneres shop at Gander Mountain? She doesn't like Dick's!

What is the main cause of pedophilia? "THOSE DAMN SEXY CLOTHES THAT THE KIDS WEAR!"

A guy asks a girl, "Did you hear about the accident on the 'cock way'?" She responds, "No, what's the 'cock way'?" He shouts out, "About a pound and a half!"

Did you hear about the new movie called, 'Constipation'? It hasn't come out yet.

I was having sex with a girl the other night. She kept calling out some other guy's name! Who the hell is 'Rape'?

Charlie Sheen opened up his own machinist's shop. It's called, 'Touch My Tool and Die'!

What do you call Charlie Sheen on roller skates? 'Rolaids'.

What was the main objective of the Jewish football game? To get the quarterback.

How do you keep an Amish girl happy? Two 'Mennonite!'

A proctologist walks into a staff meeting with a rectal thermometer tucked behind his ear. A co-worker asks him, "Why do you have a thermometer tucked behind your ear?" The proctologist replies, "Dammit! Some asshole has my pen!"

Go ahead, call the cops. You know who's going to come first!

Excuses to hit someone in the scrotum:
    "Are you tired? Time to hit the SACK!" SMACK!
    "Do you have a sleeping BAG? Time to wake it up!" SMACK!
    "What's the capital of Thailand? BANGKOK!" SMACK!

What do you call an empty bottle of Jack Daniels in the ditch? An Indian artifact. What do you call a half full bottle of Jack Daniels in the ditch? A 'rare' Indian artifact!

Why did the Indian cross the road? To pass out in the ditch!

What's the difference between a tire and 365 used condoms? One is a Good-Year, and the other is a great year!

What do you call one-thousand cattle masturbating in a field? Beef-stroken-off!

What do a Rubik's Cube and a penis have in common? The more that you play with them, the harder they get!

Are you into fitness? Try FIT-N-THIS dick in your mouth!

What time did Sean Connery go to Wimbledon? "Tennish!"

Did you hear about the Newphy who got lost while playing hockey on the Saint Lawrence River? He got a breakaway.

Why did the sperm cross the road? I put on the wrong sock this morning!

How many dead hookers does it take to change a lightbulb? Apparently more than three, my basement light is still out!

What do you call a deer with no eyes? 'NO EYE DEER!' (With your palms up and shoulders shrugging.)

What did the vet say to the dog that kept licking his balls? "THANKS!"

What do Italians call an Italian fog? "A BIGAMIST!"

What do you call an Italian astronaut? "A SPECIMEN!"

Have you read the book, 'Chinese Rupture", written by Won Hung Lo.

A guy is walking along the beach when he sees a girl with no arms and no legs, and she seems upset. He approaches her and asks her, "What's wrong?" She responds, "I have no arms and no legs, and I've never been hugged before." So, the guy decides to pick her up and give her a hug and then he walks on. The girl then starts crying, so the guy goes back and asks her, "What's wrong now?" She says, "I have no arms and no legs, and I've never been kissed before." So, the guy picks her up and kisses her and then he walks on. She then starts bawling her eyes out. He goes back, annoyed, and asks, "What the hell now?" She says, "I have no arms and no legs, and I've never been fucked before." So, the guy picks her up and throws her into the lake and he says, "Now you're fucked!"

How do you keep a retard in suspense? I'll tell you tomorrow!

What did Stevie wonder say when he walked into the bar? "OUCH!"

What do you throw a drowning Ethiopian? A CHEERIO!

What are an Indians two favorite colours? 'Blue' and 'Blue Light'

How many potatoes does it take to kill an Irishman? None! (The potato famine)

What's the difference between and Irish wedding and an Irish funeral? One less drunk!

Did you hear about the two gay Irishmen? Henry Fitzpatrick and Patrick Fitzhenry!

What do you call a gay Scotsman? 'Gay-lick!'

What do you call a gay Jew? 'He-blew!'

What time was the Chinaman's dentist appointment? 'Tooth-hurty!'

How many Jewish mothers does it take to screw in a lightbulb? None. "You all go out and have fun, I'll just sit here in the dark!"

What's the difference between 'Jam' and 'Jelly'? You can't 'Jelly' you cock down a girl's throat!

What do you call a fish with no eye? A 'FSH!'

What do they do to every 'Tickle-Me-Elmo' doll before they put in the box and ship it away from the factory? They give it two test tickles!

In 1974, Who hit the most home runs? Hank Aaron. In 1974, which batter struck out the most at the plate? Hank Aaron. In 1974, who got hit by the most balls in the face? Rock Hudson!

What do you call a woman who wears flip-flops in the winter? FAT!

I was lying in bed with my girlfriend the other day when she called me a 'Pedophile'. I told her that that was a really big word for a nine-year-old!

What do you do when your dishwasher stops working? You slap the bitch!

What do you call a woman who doesn't know how to make a sandwich? SINGLE!

How many A.D.H.D. kid's does it take to screw in a lightbulb? Want to go ride BIKES??!!

Every time that I kiss my wife after I've taken Omega-3 fish oil pills she thinks that I've been cheating on her!

What do you call a man with no arms and no legs sitting in a caldron surrounded by cannibals? STU!

How do you starve a welfare recipient? Hide his welfare check under his work boots!

Why do they give bed-ridden men Viagra in nursing homes? So, they won't roll out of bed!

I'm taking Viagra for my sunburn. It doesn't cure the problem, but it keeps the sheets off of my legs while I sleep!

I didn't know what to wear to my 'Premature ejaculation support group'. I just came in my pants.

What's the difference between anal sex and regular sex? Regular sex can make your day, but anal sex can make your hole weak!

Knock, knock. Who's there? I eat mop. I eat mop who? That's gross, go brush your teeth!

What's strong enough for a man but made for a woman? The back of my hand!

What sound do Italian tires make when they go flat? Dago "WOP, WOP, WOP!"

What's the worst part about locking your keys in the car in front of the abortion clinic? Having to go inside and ask for a coat-hanger!

What do you call a two-legged cow? YOUR MOM!

If I wanted to hear from an asshole, I'd fart.

What do you call a lesbian with thick fingers? WELL HUNG!

A guy asks his buddy, "Do you know about reverse psychology?" His buddy says, "No." "Then you probably don't want to hear this joke."

There are these two naked statues of a man and a woman standing across from each other in a secluded park. After a few hundred years of standing across the park from each other and being in constant eye contact, an angel flies down to meet the two statues. With a wave of the angel's hand, the two statues are given life and they step down from their pedestals. The angel says to them, "I have been sent to grant the mutual requests that you both have made after standing and staring at each other, unable to move. But you must proceed with haste, you both only have fifteen minutes before you become statues again. The man looks at the woman, and they both blush, giggle, and run off into the bushes. After the sound of intense rustling from the bushes for about seven minutes, they both return to the angel, satisfied. The angel smiles at the couple and asks, "That was only seven minutes, why not go back into the bushes and do it again?" The woman statue asks the males statue, "Sounds good to me, but how about this time, you hold down the pigeon, and I'll shit on it!"

What do you do when your wife starts smoking? Slow down your pace and get some K-Y Jelly!

What did the horny frog say? "RUBBIT!"

Did you hear about the constipated accountant? He couldn't budget, so he had to work it out with a pencil and paper!

What's the speed limit in bed? 68, because if you hit 69, you have to turn around!

What do you do when you come across an elephant in the jungle? Wipe your cum off of him and tell him very apologetically that you're sorry!

Why didn't Tigger flush the toilet? Because when he looked inside, he saw Pooh!

Why can't Miss Piggy count to 100? Because every time that she gets to 69, she gets a frog in her throat!

Why do midgets laugh while they're playing soccer? Because the grass tickles their balls!

What's brown and sticky? A stick!

How do you help a constipated person? Kidnap them, take them out to a remote forest while holding an axe and scare the shit out of them!

Why are crippled people always picked on? Because they can't stand up for themselves!

What's worse than spiders on your piano? Crabs on your organ!

What did the Alabama sheriff say about the black guy who had been shot fifteen times? "It's the worst case of suicide that I have ever seen!"

Statistics show that 9 out of 10 people enjoy gang rape!

Why did Hitler commit suicide? He got the gas bill!

What did the fish say when he swam into a wall? "DAM!"

What was Forrest Gump's password? 1forrest1

An old married couple are in church on a Sunday. The old woman tells her husband, "I just let out a long and silent fart. What should I do? ". The husband says, "You should replace the batteries in your hearing aids!"

What does a nosey pepper do? It gets Jalapeno business!

Who makes more money, a drug dealer, or a hooker? A hooker, she can wash her crack and resell it!

How many Emo kids does it take to screw in a lightbulb? None, they all sit in the dark and cry!

Why is it hard for girls to play hockey? Because they have to change their pads every period!

Knock, knock. Who's there? I suck. I suck who? Michael Jackson.

What do you call an Ethiopian with a yeast infection? A quarter pounder with cheese!

Did you hear about the dyslexic devil worshipper? He sold his soul to Santa!

How do you circumcise a redneck? Kick his sister in the chin!

How do you stop a dog from humping your leg? Pick him up and suck his cock!

What is the difference between erotic and kinky? Erotic is using a feather, kinky is using the whole chicken!

What did the cannibal do after he dumped his girlfriend? He wiped his ass!

Knock, knock. Who's there? Dozer. Dozer who? Dozer the biggest tits that I've ever seen!

What's faster than a Puerto Rican running away from the police with a T.V.? His brother running away with the XBOX ONE console!

How do you make a tissue dance? Put 'a little boogie' in it!

What do you call a man with a micro-penis? Justin!

Why was the guitar teacher arrested? For fingering A-minor!

Did you get those yoga pants on sale? Because at my house, they're 100% off!

What do walruses and Tupperware have in common? They both like a tight seal!

Why do women have small feet? So that they can stand closer to the sink!

Why do Sumo wrestlers shave their legs? Because they don't want to be confused with feminists!

How do you make you wife scream during sex? After you're done coming, wipe your dick off on the curtains!

What are redneck instructions for putting on underwear? Yellow up front, brown in the back!

What's a good redneck pickup line? Nice tooth!

How do you slow down a hooker? Put a governor on her (Elliot Spitzer).

Why do they call PMS 'PMS'? Because Mad Cow Disease was already taken!

Why do Scotsmen like to have sex with their sheep at the edge of a cliff? The sheep push back harder that way!

How does a Jew make coffee? Hebrews it!

A patient walks into a psychiatrist's office wearing nothing but Saran Wrap around his midsection. The doctor looks up from his paperwork and says, "I can clearly see you're nuts!"

How do Jamaicans commit suicide? They stick their heads out of a moving car window and let their lips beat them to death!

What do you throw a drowning lawyer? His wife and his kids!

A proctologist walks into a staff meeting with a rectal thermometer tucked behind his ear. A co-worker asks him, "Why do you have a thermometer tucked behind your ear?" The proctologist replies, "Dammit! Some asshole has my pen!"

The procrastinators meeting has been rescheduled until tomorrow.

Dyslexics of the world, "UNTIE!"

What did the Indian girl say when she lost her virginity? "Get off of me, Dad, you're crushing my smokes!"

PMS jokes aren't funny. Period!

How do you know if you're at a gay picnic? The hotdogs taste like shit!

Did you hear about the guy that had his left arm and leg amputated after a car crash? He's alright now!

What's the difference between a bunch of circus midgets and a girl's high school track team? The circus midgets are a bunch of cunning little runts...

What do you call a hooker with a runny nose? Full!

Apparently, heroin addicts spend upwards of $500 dollars a day. On an unrelated note, does anyone want to lend me $500 dollars?

Girls always want guys to chase them. But apparently when I'm running behind them with a knife in my hand, it's inappropriate!

What borders on stupidity? Canada and Mexico!

I remember my fist kiss with Liz. It was during recess by the swings. I grabbed her face and kissed her awkwardly for about ten seconds. That night, the kiss was all that I could think about. But apparently, she told her parents. That's why I'm not allowed to be a teacher in New York state anymore!

Apparently, "Showering her with love" doesn't mean coming on her while she's sleeping!

My fat girlfriend demanded that, for her birthday, I get her something that goes from 0 to 200 in five seconds. Apparently, a scale wasn't something that she was expecting!

A barber got arrested today for dealing drugs and running an escort service. It's crazy how you've known someone for years and then you find out their secret life after all. I never knew that he was a barber!

What do you get when you convince a gorilla to have sex with a pig? Fired from the zoo!

I got fired from my job as a teacher today for sending a student to the principle for being "tardy". Apparently, that is unacceptable behavior for a special-ed teacher!

I intend to live forever. So far, so good!

I used to work at a fire hydrant factory. You couldn't park anywhere near the place!

When everything is coming your way, you're in the wrong lane!

What is a Jewish girl's favorite wine? "I want to go to Florida!"

The Italian says, "I'm tired and thirsty, I must have wine!"
The Frenchman says, "I'm tired and thirsty, I must have cognac!"
The Russian says, "I'm tired and thirsty, I must have vodka!"
The German says, "I'm tired and thirsty, I must have beer!"
The Mexican says, "I'm tired and I'm thirsty. I must have Tequila!"
The Jew says, "I'm tired and thirsty, I must have diabetes!

What do fat girls and mopeds have in common? They're both fun to ride until your friends find out!

What's the difference between a baby and a sandwich? I don't rape a sandwich before I cut it in half and eat it!

I failed my biology exam today. When they asked, "What's commonly found in cells?", apparently "Puerto-Ricans" wasn't the correct answer!

What's the difference between dark humour and a kid with cancer? Neither one of them gets old!

How do you know if a girl is too young for you? It's when you pretend that your cock is an aero plane, and you fly it into her mouth.

What do you get when you 'Blend' a baby? An erection!

How many babies does it take to paint a wall red? One, if you throw it hard enough!

I ruined the mojo of my workout this morning. I was doing naked pushups, but I didn't see the mousetrap!

A Chinaman gets a new job on a ship. On his first day, the foreman asks him to go below the deck and get ready for the supplies. About two hours go by and no one has seen the Chinaman anywhere. The foreman gathers his crew, and they scour the lower deck looking for him. They all figured that the Chinaman must have gone overboard. They start walking towards the steps to go back above deck and out from behind a crate jumps the Chinaman and he yells. "Supplies!"

My wife is so fat that when she lays on the beach, people feel sorry for her and try to push her back into the water!

Your mom is so stupid that it takes her 2 hours to watch 60 minutes!

What do Ethiopians do at night? They starve!

This year I want to have a traditional Thanksgiving. I'm going to invite all of my neighbours to my house, give them a huge feast and then kill them and take all of their land!

Always give one hundred percent. Unless you're donating blood!

My Mexican friend's mother died. Every time that I see him now, I say, "MUCHO". It means a lot to him!

Why did the Mexican take Xanax? For Hispanic Attacks.

What do priests and Michael Jackson have in common? They both stick their meat in ten-year-old buns!

An obese woman goes to a doctor and gets put on a drastic weight-loss program. The doctor tells her that she can eat anything that she wants, but all of the food must be inserted into her anus. The woman agrees to this and returns four weeks later for a checkup. The doctor is very pleased with the woman's weight loss, but he's concerned about her hips, which were constantly twitching. "When did your hips start to twitch?" asks the doctor. The woman replies, "I'm not twitching! I'm just chewing gum!"

Today was a really bad day. My mother-in-law got hit by a cab AND I lost my job as a cab driver!

Today, I smoked so much weed today that I got more stoned today than a Saudi Arabian rape victim!

A son asks his dad, "Why is my sister named Rose?" His dad replies, "Because your mom likes Roses. But you already knew that, Cocaine!"

My wife is worried because I have an addiction to brake fluid. I told her, "I can stop at any time!"

The doctor told my wife that she can't touch anything alcoholic. Now she's divorcing me!

When my wife discovered that I had replaced our bed with a trampoline, SHE HIT THE ROOF!

I was struggling to put on my seatbelt and then, "It just clicked!"

My dad told me to stop walking in circles. I wouldn't comply so he nailed my other foot to the floor!

I came home early from work one day and I saw a guy jogging down the street in his underwear. I asked him, "Why are you jogging in your underwear?" He said to me, "You came home from work early!"

What's an Ethiopian's favorite book? "My life and other short stories."

How do you start an Ethiopian rave? Nail a sandwich to the ceiling!

What's something that both an Ethiopian and an American can never have? Just one potato chip!

Have you ever had Ethiopian food? Neither have Ethiopians.

What was the score of the Ethiopian baseball game? Eight nothing!

What's the difference between a pair of jeans and an Ethiopian? A pair of jeans has only one fly on it!

I'm staying in a hotel right now. There's no 13th floor because of superstition. But really, the people on the 14th floor should know that they're jinxed!

I don't have a girlfriend. I just know that a girl that would be really mad at me if she heard me say that!

At my lemonade stand I used to give the first glass away for free. Then I would charge 5 dollars for the second glass. The second glass contained the antidote!

I got into a fight with a really big and tough guy the other day. He said, "I'm going to mop the floor with your face!" I said, "you'll be sorry!" He said, Oh yeah, why?" I said, "Well, you won't be able to get into the corners very well!"

I love to go down to the schoolyard and watch all of the little children jump up and down and run around yelling and screaming! They don't know that I'm only using blanks in my gun!

I once had a large gay following, but then I ducked into an alleyway and lost him!

I used to be addicted to soap...but I'm clean now!

A farmer buys a new rooster that turns out to be a sex maniac. It tears around, mating with all of the chickens, ducks, geese, and the turkeys. The rooster even tried to have sex with the farm cat. After a week of the rooster having frantic sex, the farmer finds the bird lying flat on its back, eyes closed, with a couple of vultures circling over him. The farmer says, "I knew that your heart would give out sooner or later, you sex maniac!" The rooster opens up one eye, looks up at the vultures and says to the farmer, "Shut up and get lost! You're going to scare my new girlfriends away!"

My mother was like a sister to me. Although, we didn't have sex quite as often!

What do you call ten Ethiopians carrying a canoe over their heads? A comb!

"Please cooperate, otherwise it's going to look like rape!"

Here's an old Ethiopian proverb. "You can't have your cake or eat it!"

Rape is terrible! I'll never understand how a man can traumatize a woman like that. That's why I always make sure that I give my women roofies!

I want to hang a map of the world in my house. Then I'm going to put pins into all of the locations that I've travelled to. But first, I'm going to have to travel to the top two corners of the map, so it won't fall down!

What did one menstrual vampire say to the other? "My pad or yours?"

Why don't rednecks do 'reverse cowgirl?' Because they never turn their backs on their family!

You're the cum-shot that your mom wanted to swallow but your dad couldn't pull out in time!

I like to hide my girlfriend's asthma inhaler from her, so my neighbours think that I'm a stud when they hear her panting and saying, "Give it to me!"

Why did God give men penises? So, they'd have at least one way to shut a woman up!

A little catholic boy asks his priest, "Do you mind if I play the organ this week?" The priest replies, "No, not at all!"

What do you say to a blonde with no arms and no legs? Nice tits!

My wife is six months pregnant. The nurses asked me if I wanted to put my hand on the baby. Apparently, they meant from the outside!

What did one boob say to the other? You are my breast friend!

Why don't policemen get Mad Cow Disease? Because they're all pigs!

My new favorite sexual position is called, "WOW!" It's when I flip your 'MOM' over and fuck her!

What do you call an Ethiopian walking a dog? A vegetarian!

What do you say to a woman with two black eyes? Nothing! You already told her twice!

What do all battered women have in common? THEY JUST DON' T LISTEN!!!!!!

What's better than winning the Special Olympics? Not being retarded!

Your mom is so fat that when she sat on her iPhone, it turned into and iPad!

What's the difference between an ISIS training camp and elementary school? I don't know, I'm only eight years old. I just fly drones!

A man walks into a crowded doctor's office and says loudly to the receptionist, "There's something wrong with my penis!" The receptionist looks up and says, "You shouldn't say things like that in a public area. Please leave, and when you come back, say that there's something wrong with your ear, or something like that." The man leaves the waiting room and waits a for a minute, and then re-enters. He says to the receptionist, "There's something wrong with my ear." She asks, "What's wrong with your ear?" The man says, "It really hurts when I piss out of it!"

I ran into Hitler the other day. He said, "I'm going to kill 6 million Jews and two clowns." I asked, why are you going to kill two clowns?" He said, "Seeeee, nobody cares about zee Jews!"

So, I was raping this girl the other night and she said, "Please think about my children!" What a kinky bitch!

I told my girlfriend that she would look a lot sexier with her hair back. Apparently, that's a cruel thing to say to a cancer patient.

How do you know if Michael Jackson is having a party? All of the 'Big Wheels' in his front yard!

I got in trouble with my wife at dinner last night. Apparently, when she asked me to turn on the veg, fingering her disabled sister wasn't what she meant!

What's worse than eating your grandmother's pussy? Banging the back of your head on the lid of her coffin!

A man goes to the corner store. He asks the girl at the counter, "Can I have a 'Kit Kat Chunky?'" The girl goes and gets him a Kit Kat Chunky. The man shouts, "NOOO!! I wanted a normal Kit Kat, you fat cunt!"

My boss touched me inappropriately at work today. It's ok though, I'm self-employed!

The more that I practice boxing, the more unclear and obscure the things around me are!

I have an exceptional butt. Every time that I walk away from a conversation, people say, "What an ass!"

You're Mama's so stupid that when she went to mandarin class she asked, "Where are the Mandarins, I'm starving!"

I googled a 'Rorschach' test for some reason. All that came up were pictures of my parents fighting!

Why do Italian guys have moustaches? So, they can look 'Justa-like-mama!"

I've been trying to form a 'Sarcastic club'. It's been really hard to tell if people are interested in joining or not!

Working in a mirror factory is something that I can totally see myself doing!

What's the difference between a dead hooker and your job? Your job still sucks.

Wise words from Corky Thatcher, "Don't let an extra chromosome get you down!"

Did you hear about the Ethiopian who fell into a river full of piranhas? He ate half of them before they could pull him out!

What goes, "clop-clop, bang-bang, clop-clop, bang-bang? An Amish drive by shooting!

Two Irishmen walk by a sign that reads, "TREE FELLERS WANTED." The one Irishman says to the other, "Too bad there's only two of us fellers".

Why can't two Chinese people have a white baby? Because two Wong's don't make a white?

Why was Hellen Keller's leg yellow? Because her dog was blind too!

Why do Mexican cars have small steering wheels? So, they can still drive with handcuffs on!

What do you call a Chinese rapist? Rai Ping Yu!

Why does Hellen Keller masturbate with just one hand? So, she can moan with the other!

Why are Ethiopians good at blowjobs? Because they swallow everything that they eat!

Why don't vampires like garlic? You have to exist to dislike garlic!

What's the oddest thing that you can think of? Numbers that can't be divided by two!

How can you tell if it's sunny outside? By looking out of the window, you idiot!

What's a pirate's favorite letter? There isn't one because scientists believe that most pirates were illiterate in their time!

What's worse than finding a worm in your apple? Choking on your apple!

What is the most frightening word in nuclear physics? "OOPS!"

How did the magician make the pizza disappear? He ate it!

I'll never forget what my grandpa said before he kicked the bucket, "Hey, do you want to see how far I can kick this bucket?"

What did Batman say to Robin when they got into the Batmobile? "Robin, get into the Batmobile!"

Who is Bill Cosby's favorite princess? Sleeping Beauty!

A cowboy rides into town and hitches his horse to a post. He then lifts his horse's tail and kisses the horse's asshole. An old-timer is watching and asks, "Why did you kiss your horse's asshole?" The cowboy replies, "It help my chapped lips." "You mean that kissing a horse's ass cures chapped lips?" The cowboy responds, "It doesn't cure them, but it sure stops me from licking them!"

Losing a wife is very tough. I've been trying to do it for years and it's nearly impossible!

This year for lent, I'm giving up being Jewish!

Why are there no Mexicans in the Olympics? Because anyone of them who can run, jump, or swim is already in America!

I bought you a calendar. Your days are numbered!

Two stoners are having a chat and the one stoner asks his buddy, "When is your birthday?" His buddy says, "December 12th." The other stoner asks, "What year?" His buddy says, "Every year!"

Where there's a will, there's a dead relative.

If it's unhealthy to eat late at night, then why is there a light in the fridge!?

I gave up my seat on the bus for a blind person. It cost me my job as a bus driver!

Time flies like an arrow. Fruit flies like a banana!

Why was Helen Keller's dog blind? Because she used to feed it with a fork!

What's the difference between my dead grandma and onions? I cried when I cut up the onions!

What's the difference between me and cancer? My dad didn't beat cancer!

A dog walks into a post office and says to the postmaster, "I need to send a telegram." The postmaster says, "Okay, what is it?" The dog says, "I need it to say, 'woof, woof, woof, woof, woof, woof, woof!'" The postmaster counts the words and says, "Well, for the same price, I can put three more 'woofs' in the telegram for you." The dog looks at him and says, "But then it wouldn't make any sense!"

What's the worst thing that your sibling can steal from you? Your virginity!

What has four legs and a hand? A lion in a daycare center!

Your mom is so fat that when she stepped on a scale, the scale said, 'help!'

Why does grandma like gardening so much? Because she loves getting dirty and down on her knees!

What do you call Snoop Dog in a hot air balloon? Higher than usual!

Where can you never take an orphan? A family restaurant!

I had a crush on my teacher which was confusing, because I was homeschooled.

Even people that are good for nothing have the capacity to bring a smile to your face. For example, when you push them down the stairs!

A guy has a few too many drinks at the bar and then gets into his car. He gets pulled over and is arrested by a beautiful and busty female police officer. She arrests him for DWI and says to him, "You are under arrest. Anything that you say can and will be held against you." He blurts out, "BOOBS!"

For sale: A parachute. Used just once, never opened, it just has a small stain.

I childproofed my house. Somehow, they still got in!

What do you call people who use the 'rhythm method' for contraception? Parents!

Why are cigarettes good for the environment? Because they kill people!

What do you call two Mexicans playing basketball against each other? Juan on Juan.

I've spent the past two years looking for my ex-girlfriend's killer. For the life of me, I can't find anyone to do the job!'

Two brunettes and a blonde work in the same office with the same female boss. They notice that the boss always leaves work early so one day they decide to leave work right after she does. The two brunettes go for coffee, but the blonde decides to go home and surprise her husband. When she gets to her house she sneaks inside and hears noises from the bedroom. Peering in through the bedroom door she sees her boss in bed with her husband. Horrified, she creeps away. The next day at the office the brunettes suggest leaving early again. "No way!" says the blonde. "Yesterday I almost got caught!"

Why did Helen Keller wear skintight pants? So, you could read her lips!

The proof that humans don't truly understand death is that we still give dead people a pillow!

Swimming is very healthy for you, especially if you're drowning. Not only do you get a good cardiovascular workout, but you also won't die!

What breed of dog can jump higher than a skyscraper? Any breed, skyscrapers can't jump!

Why can't Hellen Keller have kids? Because she's dead!

Why did Adele cross the road? To say, 'Hello from the other side!"

How do you know if it's bedtime at Michael Jackson's house? When the big hand touches the little hand!

Why is it that if you donate a kidney, people love you? But if you donate five kidneys, then people call the police!

How many Mexicans does it take to grease your car? Just one, if you hit him hard enough!

An American man is in Hong Kong and has sex with a prostitute. After a wild night of sex, the man wakes up and finds that his dick is covered in green spots and that it hurt's like hell! He rushes to the top western doctor in Hong Kong and shows the doctor his dick. The doctor says, "This is a rare Chinese disease, but common amongst our native prostitutes. Unfortunately, the cure is to amputate your penis." The man goes to get a second opinion from another western doctor who gives him the same diagnosis. The man then decides to see a traditional Chinese doctor. The man says, "Doctor, I need your help! Take a look at my penis. All of the other doctors tell me that I have to amputate it! Can you help me, please?" The Chinese doctor examines the man's penis and says, "Stupid American doctors always want to amputate, they want more money! No need to amputate." The man says, with relief, "Thank God!" The Chinese doctor says, "Your penis will fall off by itself!"

A son asks his dad, "Dad. Did you get the paternity DNA test results back yet?" The dad says, "Don't call me dad anymore, call me George!"

Why didn't Helen Keller's son have any ears? Because she gave him his first haircut!

How did Helen Keller's parents punish her? Either they put the toilet seat on the stove, re-arranged the furniture, ran on her brail with golf shoes, left the plunger in the toilet or put doorknobs on the walls!

British scientists have demonstrated that cigarettes can harm your children. That makes sense, use an ashtray to put out your smokes instead!

Why did Helen Keller's dog run away? You would too if your name was, "Oooggggghhhhhaarrrgghh."

I asked a very pretty, homeless girl if I could take her home. She smiled and said, "Yes!" But then she got very upset when I walked off with her cardboard box.

What do K-mart and Michael Jackson have in common? They both have little boy's pants half off!

Two stoners are up late one night in their apartment. The first guy asks his friend, "What time is it?" His buddy responds, "I'm not sure, but hand me that trombone over there and I'll let you know." The first guy asks, "How the hell can you tell the time with a trombone?" The second guy bursts out a long and loud note on the trombone. He then stops, waits, and listens. Suddenly, a loud voice screams from the apartment above, "Who the hell is playing the trombone at 3 AM in the morning!?"

Made in the USA
Las Vegas, NV
15 April 2023

70643948R00077